Secrets in Brierley Bramble

J.P. Stringer

Skip

Madam Pom

Piggy Mama

Alfie

Little Rufus

Hazel

A further tale of Guinea Pigs, Nature and Magic

Brierley Bramble UK
© J.P. Stringer 2021

Illustrations by Natasa Devic
(some based on original concepts by Kim Fowler)

Cover design & illustration by Adrian Doan Kim

Book layout and design by Glenn at fiverr.com/sarco2000

ISBN 978-1-8381321-2-5

With love for those who make my world so special
Jim, Robb, Will & Eve
Sarah, Ian, Isabel & Christopher
Sasha & Lola
Dusty, Bear, Pippin,
Womble & Chestnut

and for
Lorna
Reece, Aoife
Colin & Frankie
&
Rumble
If only you could have stayed with us for longer

Love also to our youngest stars
Ella & Alex
Daniel, Oliver & William
Marshall, Ryan & Callum
Olivia, William, Isabella & Eloisa
Keilan, Ryker, Rocco & Alexa
Marcus & Malachi
Harvey & Elsie
Remi & Lois

'If you can be anything in this world, be kind.'
Caroline Flack

Contents

A small reminder of the story so far

THE story takes place in the English village of Brierley Bramble, where Hazel the guinea pig lives with Piggy Mama, plus her younger brothers, Alfie and Little Rufus.

The piggies were rescued from a life of neglect by a kind older lady, called Betty. Through a series of events, involving a Moon Wish placed by Hazel, they found a new home with the Greenwood family (John and his children, Billy and Molly) in a house named Bowood, on the edge of the village.

Two Pomeranians, by the name of Madam Pom and Skip, live there too.

When the Full Moon comes each month, the animals meet with The Moon Queen, who rules over the garden, and her sprites: Godfrig, Merriel, Oro and Fion. They are spirits of earth, water, air and fire.

During daylight hours, The Moon Queen and her sprites live as small marble statuettes beneath a silver birch tree, at the bottom of the Bowood garden. After dark, the sprites transform and appear either as fairy-like figures or orbs of light. Only when the Full Moon is in the sky, does the Moon Queen's statuette change.

One of the Moon Queen's first gifts to Hazel was to ride on the back of a heron, so she could see the world from up on high. Her second gift to Hazel was the ability to walk on her back legs.

Unlike the other animals at Bowood, the small guinea pig is able to understand fully what the humans say. This capability was inherited from a very special ancestor, named Grama Lizzy.

We last saw Hazel dancing in the rain, whilst a silver hare watched from a distance.

Chapter 1
Pea Flakes

A WARM current of air passed over the village of Brierley Bramble, and lifted the outspread wings of Blake the heron as he soared through the crystal blue sky.

Sitting on his back, between his soft grey wings, was Hazel the guinea pig. The early summer sunshine warmed her back whilst she gazed down upon the world she loved.

In the heart of Brierley Bramble, far below, young children chattered and played on the village green, some chasing in a game of tig, others making daisy chains, holding buttercups beneath their chins or blowing dandelion clocks.

The doors to the many shops each stood open wide to welcome in passers-by for a purchase or a chat.

Mrs Adebayo, the chemist, was sunbathing in her doorway; Mr Singh, the florist, was arranging roses in the window; and Ernie Bostock was setting out brooms, buckets and other sundry goods in front of his hardware store, as the fringe on the sunshade above his head gently flapped.

On the roof of the junior school, the rooster weathervane twirled joyfully, as if to celebrate the beautiful day Nature had provided.

In the cottage gardens, lines of washing danced upon the breeze. Tee shirts and socks of every shade and hue frolicked and capered beside pretty pastel sun dresses and brightly coloured shorts, whilst sparkling white sheets caught the air and billowed like the sails on a ship.

Cycling along in the sunshine was P.C. Frankie, returning home from his early morning ride. As he passed the garden of Betty Albright's cottage, he gave a cheery wave to the lady herself. She could be seen laying out fresh plants and flowers to dry, after a morning's foraging in Lundy Woods.

By the edge of the village, in the flower meadows of Bowood, Billy Greenwood was lying on his back, contemplating life, with a strand of sweet grass between his teeth, and Skip the small orange Pomeranian sitting faithfully by his side.

As the heron and the guinea pig passed over the elegant silver birch tree, at the bottom of the Bowood garden, they spotted Mr Greenwood chiselling wood in the open doorway of his workshop. Madam Pom, the pedigree Pomeranian, snoozed peacefully in the shade, where Molly Greenwood also sat with a sketchpad upon her knee.

Knowing they must not be seen by humans, Blake avoided the lawn, where the white marble statuettes of The Moon Queen and her sprites stood in their circle, and headed instead for the orchard on the other side of the hedge.

Once the heron had made a smooth landing in a clearing between the trees, Hazel slipped out from the thick twist of vine which held her on his back, and thanked him politely, as always.

Bidding him farewell, she made her way to the hole in the wall behind the camellia bush, practising her new-found ability to walk on her two back legs along the way.

Once inside, she walked on all fours across the floor of the outhouse, over to the guinea pig hutch where her family lived, and squeezed her way in through the lifted corner of the wire run beneath. Here she found Alfie, Little Rufus and Piggy Mama in deep discussion.

It was all about pea flakes.

Or rather, the lack of them. For the past week or so, there had been little sign of the precious green delicacies in the piggies' dried food bowls.

Each member of the family had their own particular preference. Hazel favoured the dried apple pieces, Alfie had a soft spot for the crushed maize and Little Rufus particularly enjoyed the oats, whilst Piggy Mama was happiest with the timothy hay nuggets.

Mama would often scold her brood for picking out only the sweet bits they liked, leaving behind the nutritious nuggets. "That's what they call *selective feeding*," she would say sternly, "and it is not good for you. You're often too full to eat enough hay."

One thing enjoyed by all, however, was a nice crunchy pea flake. Even Mama would give in to temptation on occasions and nibble happily on the tasty green treats when the fancy took her.

The trouble was that there were fewer and fewer pea flakes appearing in the dried food bowls just lately, causing much grumbling and discontent amongst Hazel and her piggy brothers. They had tried wheeking at Billy when he dished up their food, but of course, he did not understand. Whilst Hazel could decipher humans' words (thanks to an inherited ability from her ancestor, Grama Lizzy) she could not talk back to them.

"Do you think they're too expensive?" asked Alfie.

Hazel had once explained the concept of money to her brother, as her understanding of the human language gave her insights into the human world, not open to the others.

"No," Hazel assured him. "I think Our Boy Billy must have just changed the food."

Once breakfast was over, the piggies retired for a snooze. They each had a preferred place to sleep. Hazel and Alfie liked to be on the lower level of the hutch, closer to the run and freedom, whilst Mama cared more for the main upstairs nest box, where Rufus would often snuggle up by her side.

Recently, however, Little Rufus had taken to sleeping in the separate wooden hideaway, on the top floor, leaving Mama to sleep alone. As mothers must, she had accepted this as a sign of his growing independence and need for his own space, though it did tug at her heart just a little.

It was all part of a new behaviour from the youngest guinea pig. He was spending more and more time alone in the hideaway, coming out only for meal times. Alfie had grumbled about it as he was missing his partner in mischief, but Mama had instructed him and Hazel to ignore this behaviour for now as it was probably just a passing phase.

On this particular morning, Little Rufus had unexpectedly crept back to share his mother's warmth in the nesting box. A bad dream had taken him right back to the horrid, cold, damp hutch owned by the Bray family at 12 Oakfield Lane, and now he couldn't sleep.

This turned out well for Hazel as she had just had a quarrel with Alfie over hogging all the space in the nest box below, and for breathing too noisily in her ear.

She wanted a bit of peace and quiet, so took herself off upstairs. Finding Little Rufus's favourite wooden house empty for once, she decided to have her nap in there.

As she entered, she felt a strange crunching sensation beneath her paws. She nudged aside some of the soft hay to investigate. To her surprise, there was a pea flake hidden beneath. She lifted further strands of hay to find more and more of them. So, they *had* been getting pea flakes – but Little Rufus had been hoarding them away!

This explained his tendency to be up so early when the food bowls were being filled. The others didn't stir till the fresh food was served up by Billy. They were happy to wait till their breakfast, of tasty fresh celery leaves, chunks of refreshing cucumber, or slivers of tangy cherry tomato, was placed on the top floor of the hutch. The dried food was for munching on later in the day, along with the soft hay.

Amazed at what she had just discovered, Hazel was about to shout for Alfie, when a thought occurred to her. The boys might well be happy play mates most of the time, but they were extremely competitive too, especially where food was concerned. It would lead to a terrible bout of bickering between the brothers if the secret was to come out.

She pushed back the hay and went to consult Mama.

Chapter 2
The Foolish Wood Mouse

"Rufus," said Hazel, as she entered the nest box where Mama and her brother were sleeping, "I think Our Boy Billy is about to put some lovely fresh meadow hay down in the run. Why don't you get to it before Alfie takes all those tasty yellow flower heads that you like?"

She did not need to say it twice. Little Rufus was soon racing down the ramp to the run below, to stop his brother from scoffing all the good bits.

Mama listened to what Hazel had to say, and chuckled softly at the news of the pea flake discovery. She thought it over for a few moments and then told Hazel to wait until that evening. She agreed wholeheartedly that Alfie was not to know – not if they were to have any peace that day.

The piggies went on to enjoy a glorious afternoon in the garden, under Billy's watchful eye. He was not, of course, aware that they were protected within its boundaries by The Moon Queen, and so considered it his duty to keep them under close supervision at all times.

They had a wonderful time nibbling the fresh green grass, chasing each other around the lawn and scampering through the yellow plastic tunnels – for no other reason than the fact that they were there, and they could.

At one point, a slight dispute arose when Alfie found a particularly delicious strand of sweet grass to eat, and Little Rufus grabbed its opposite end to munch upon it too. Both boys nibbled as quickly as they could, until they met in the middle and bumped noses. As always, each blamed the other.

Hazel and Mama exchanged looks - their earlier decision to keep Little Rufus's pea hoard secret seemed all the more sensible now.

Eventually, they were brought inside. Each had a good sleep before waking up to a generous supper of cucumber slivers, a few strands of fresh green parsley, chunks of carrot and their particular favourite – romaine lettuce.

Once they had finished their feast, the piggies settled down together, as they often did on an evening. They were warm, clean and well fed. Life was blissful.

It was on such occasions that Mama would often recount tales from Grama Lizzy, her wise old great grandma, many times removed, whose knowledge and wisdom had been passed down through the generations.

Tonight, Mama had chosen 'The Tale of the Foolish Wood Mouse' to while away the evening. Her young ones snuggled down ready to hear the story.

"It begins," said Mama, "in a forest many, many moons ago."

"It was autumn, and the mice of the forest were busy foraging for food. They needed to build up their larders, ready for the chill of winter. For this was when the fruits, nuts and seeds that they relied upon so much would disappear. The tasty insects too would become so much harder to find in the cold, hard soil.

One wood mouse in particular, Topi, had a special talent for searching out the very finest food from around the forest. He would root around the oak trees for the plumpest acorns, hunt out the fullest seed pods from the sycamore trees and scour the hawthorns and brambles for the juiciest fruit with the finest seeds buried inside."

At this point, Mama stole a quick glance at Little Rufus to ensure he had not dozed off after his full supper. She then continued.

"Sadly, Topi did not use his talents for the good of others. He was a rather selfish mouse, who would rather go foraging in secret, never revealing to the others where he found his nutritional treasures.

If he knew where the best food lay, he would mark the spot with a sign, such as a small twig or pile of leaves, and return when others were not around. He would even risk becoming a meal himself for the tawny owls, foxes or wild boars of the forest, by venturing out near nightfall when the coast was clear of competitors.

Once he had found his tasty treats, he would transport them back to the underground burrow he shared with the other mice, via a hidden tunnel he had dug himself. There, he would hide all he had collected in his own secret larder."

Mama peeked once more at Little Rufus, exchanging a knowing look with Hazel. They could both tell that he was listening very carefully indeed.

The mother piggy resumed her story, "At last winter came and a cold, bitter one it was. As the season dragged on, the wood mice's stores began to run low, but not Topi's. His larder still bulged with seeds and nuts, for he had stored away far more than he could ever eat himself.

On a cold winter's evening, he would stay alone in his part of the burrow. By now he had blocked up the entrance to the place he occupied, cutting himself off from the rest of his kind. His secret tunnel became the only way to enter and exit his home.

Alone, Topi would feast upon his plentiful stores, growing fatter by the day. Meanwhile, his neighbours grew hungry and thin on the meagre remains of what they had left.

In fairness to Topi, he had no idea how desperate their plight had become. He no longer saw any of his relatives, friends or neighbours. The truth was, he dare not.

To safeguard his precious stockpile of food, he had to stay put in his home at all times. If he left, even for a short while, there was a danger that another creature could sniff out his precious hoard and help themselves. He could neither invite anyone in nor be invited out.

To make matters worse, he could no longer cosy up to other warm bodies at night. A pile of acorns offered little comfort in comparison.

Oftentimes, Topi would hear the other mice having fun elsewhere in the burrow. Some nights, there would be faint sounds of singing, dancing and laughter. Even when all was quiet, Topi knew he was missing out.

The wood mouse let out a deep, lonely sigh. More than anything else, he missed the general cheer of being with other mice, of having someone to talk to, even the very sound of another mouse's voice. He missed grooming a compan-ion's fur, and the pleasure of being groomed in return.

He curled up around a pile of seeds and tried to sleep.

Abruptly, out of the blue, his uneasy dreams were shattered when thunderous noises erupted all around him.

Topi leapt up just in time to escape being crushed by the huge brown shape which at that moment had crashed through the roof of his home. Fearing for his life, he scrambled down the tunnel which led to the outside world and bolted for safety.

From the confines of the tree root, beneath which he hid, he recognised the all too familiar sound of a wild boar chomping hungrily on acorns – his acorns!

The ravenous animal had caught the scent of his huge food store as it rooted around in the undergrowth, desperately searching for anything to eat. It had struck lucky and was now devouring the entire contents of Topi's larder.

Topi trembled and quaked with terror. He knew all too well that if the boar had spotted him before his escape, he would have made a tasty addition to the meal.

Within minutes, the wild boar had eaten its fill, and headed off through the trees.

Topi could only sit and stare, shocked beyond belief."

Mama checked once more that Rufus was still awake. His unsettled look left her in no doubt that he was still listening intently. She continued once more.

"The noise and commotion had attracted the attention of the other wood mice. They had left their burrow and now surrounded Topi with exclamations of surprise.

"Why, Topi, where have you been?" one asked.

"We've missed you." declared another. "We thought you'd gone away. We haven't seen you for so long!"

The unfortunate wood mouse could no longer hide what he had done. The truth came tumbling out and he confessed his crime in full to his astonished relatives, friends and neighbours.

There was silence as they took in the full details. Topi could only watch forlornly as they huddled together in discussion.

After what seemed like an eternity, the elder wood mouse stepped forward to speak on behalf of all concerned.

"Topi, we are sorry that you chose to behave in this way," he said, staring hard at the errant wood mouse. "But we all, as one, believe that you have learned your lesson the hard way."

The elder mouse paused before continuing, "You will be forgiven on this occasion, if you promise to use your talents in future for the general good of us all, instead of just yourself."

Topi stared at the ground, hardly daring to lift his eyes.

"From now on, all food you collect will be added to the communal store we all share. Then you will be welcome to come back and live in the burrow with the rest of us."

The elder mouse asked, "Do you wish to do so, Topi?"

Without hesitation, and with joy in his heart, the sorry wood mouse gratefully accepted the invitation.

That night, he slept soundly in the cosy warmth of the main burrow, back with his fellow companions. The other mice had gladly shared what little food they had, welcoming him back into their fold. The food was limited, but it tasted so much better in good company."

As the story of the wood mouse ended, Mama and Hazel checked once more on Little Rufus. The young guinea pig looked suitably downcast and thoughtful. The moral of the story had clearly not been lost on him.

All retired to bed, including Little Rufus, who disappeared quickly to his usual wooden hideaway.

Next morning, the family was awoken by Alfie exclaiming loudly, "I did it! The pea flakes are back!"

The puzzled faces and bleary eyes of Hazel and Mama were met with the explanation, "Last night, I wished on the New Moon that we'd get the pea flakes back again, and we just have. The food bowls are full of them!"

The triumphant guinea pig looked pointedly at his sister as if to say she wasn't the only one who could place Moon Wishes.

Hazel swallowed a smile and said calmly, "And to think I had to wait for a Full Moon for my wish to be granted. Perhaps you are now a Special One too, Alfie."

Alfie liked this idea very much, and went off to celebrate by eating as many pea flakes as he could, before Little Rufus got there.

Surprisingly, his little brother made no move at all to follow him. The young guinea pig had lost his worried frown from the night before, and now looked as if a great weight had been lifted from his shoulders. Grinning happily to himself, he trotted back to his wooden house for another sleep.

Next day, all members of the family were up early. Alfie waited in anticipation for Billy to enter from the kitchen, and for the food bowls to be filled up once more with the precious pea flakes.

Hazel and Mama exchanged secret smiles at Alfie's proud and expectant look. Their smiles were not to last.

As the first food bowl was topped up by Billy, he announced in a cheery voice, "No more selective feeding for you, Piglets. I'm putting you all on nuggets alone from now on!"

Which he did, except on Sundays, when the pea flakes returned as a weekly treat for all.

Chapter 3
New Neighbours on Oakfield Lane

Hazel, Alfie, Piggy Mama and Little Rufus were happily snoozing in their hutch, when they were awoken by the arrival of Betty Albright. They recognised her voice immediately, and got to their feet, wheeking with pleasure.

How they loved Betty's visits. She was the kind older lady who had rescued them from their terrible life with her neighbours, the Brays, at number 12, Oakfield Lane. If it was not for her, they would never have made it through the cold winter months. They had never forgotten her kindness, and always looked forward to seeing her. She always had a stroke around the ear and a tickle under the chin for each of them, especially Hazel.

Today was no different. Betty came into the outhouse and opened the top door of the hutch. Each piggy was fussed and stroked, before being given a tasty pile of herbs and plants that she had foraged that very morning.

Once she had greeted the guinea pigs, Betty sat down at the oak kitchen table for a chat with John Greenwood. He presented her with a steaming hot mug of tea and sat down himself.

By now, Billy and Molly had surfaced too, and had joined

them at the table. They liked Betty as much as the piggies did, and knew she would bring some weird and wonderful homemade cake for them, as she did most weekends.

As everyone tucked into a slice of courgette, basil and lime cake, Betty began to tell the Greenwoods an interesting piece of news - new neighbours had moved into the Bray's old cottage on Oakfield Lane.

"Already?" said John.

"Yes, but that's not the most surprising part," returned Betty. She went on to explain how late the previous evening, under the cover of darkness, the sound of a vehicle engine was heard pulling up at the kerbside. Betty had peeped through her curtains to see a small removal van. Items were being unloaded and taken into the cottage by a couple of men in overalls.

Full of curiosity, Betty had used her usual ploy of pretending to be out looking for an imaginary pet cat. It had been her favourite way of unnerving the Brays. It now gave her an excuse to wander out of the front door of her own cottage and 'accidentally' meet her new neighbours.

"Sheba!" she called, "Sheba!"

Billy and Molly erupted in giggles at this part of the story. However, the guinea pigs, listening in the outhouse, were still shuddering at the mention of the name *Bray*. That was one human word they *all* recognised.

Betty continued to recount that as she called out for the non-existent cat, she caught sight of a man with a walking stick. He had his back to her. "Good evening," she greeted him cheerily. "You must be my new neighbours. I'm Betty Albright."

The man spun around as if quite shocked to be spoken to. His eyes glanced nervously over to a woman in the

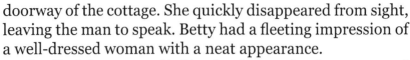

doorway of the cottage. She quickly disappeared from sight, leaving the man to speak. Betty had a fleeting impression of a well-dressed woman with a neat appearance.

"Hello," the man replied in a hesitant voice that suggested he felt a little caught out.

Betty had introduced herself once more and waited expectantly for him to do the same.

"Cecil Pepper," he said curtly. The man then attempted to be a little more friendly. "Pleased to meet you," he said, putting on a smile. "I won't stop – my wife, Hortense, has lots for me to do!" He made a gesture with his eyes towards the doorway, and gave an apologetic grin as he limped stiffly inside.

Betty stopped the story at this point for a sip of her tea, but then carried on to describe the oddest thing about the couple. Although the man's voice and smile had seemed cheerful enough, this had not extended to his eyes. The nervous look he had given the woman made Betty all the more curious. She sensed there was something not quite right. It had left her wanting to know more about the elusive woman seen briefly in the doorway.

"Have you spoken to them since?" asked John.

"No," replied Betty, "there has been no chance to."

She had looked to speak to the couple each time she came and went from her own cottage, but no opportunity to do so presented itself. Mr and Mrs Pepper were keeping very much to themselves. In the end, Betty took round a freshly baked blackberry pie (with an added twist of mint) and tapped on the door. No response came. With a resigned and puzzled sigh, Betty left it as a gift on the door step.

Billy asked, "Do you think they'll be as horrible as the Brays?"

Hazel was wondering that too, as she listened, able to understand more than the other piggies.

"I hope not," replied Betty. "This is a small community. Whoever lives here affects us all."

Little did Betty know how prophetic her words would be. The chance to meet the elusive woman would come all too soon.

Over the days that followed, they would discover that whilst the woman was a distant figure at home, when it came to village affairs, she would prove to be very different indeed.

Mrs Pepper was about to cast a shadow over the lives of many in the village of Brierley Bramble.

Chapter 4
Strife in the Greenwood Home

As a sweltering midsummer's day cooled into a warm humid evening, a delicious cool breeze gently stirred the flowers and leaves of the Bowood garden. It rippled the elegant green branches hanging from the silver birch tree, lifted the petals of the golden sunflowers, and swayed the delicate stems of the fizzy cosmos. It was the only movement in the stillness.

It should have been a perfect end to the day, but it was not.

The piggies shuddered and huddled together in their hutch, as doors were slammed, and loud voices filled the air. Molly was crying and Billy was thumping around in his room upstairs.

Mr Greenwood had gone out into his workshop to escape the tensions inside the house and was now hammering nails into a piece of wood, perhaps a little harder than was required.

Eventually, once all was calm again, the piggies crept out of the hutch and onto the outhouse floor for a discussion with Skip and Madam Pom.

"What do you think is going on?" Hazel asked Skip.

Skip visited Molly and Billy in their rooms most nights, whereas the guinea pigs where only taken up every now and again, so the orange dog might know things that they did not. Madam Pom did go upstairs on occasions, but her preferred place was by the side of Mr Greenwood. Partly because she was very fond of being near him, but also because the stairs were far too much effort.

Skip thought about Hazel's question carefully. Billy often came home from school in a bad mood, but today he had been even worse. Skip had seen him bring out a piece of paper from his schoolbag, which he had reluctantly handed to Mr Greenwood. Things seemed to have gone from there.

At this point, Madam Pom decided to contribute. She always slept on a dog bed in the outhouse during any such discussions with the guinea pigs, or at least pretended to. She generally considered conversations with them to be beneath her dignity, but was far too nosey not to listen and join in when she felt like it. "It was a *letta*," she suddenly announced, opening one eye and not bothering to raise her head from her paws.

Madam's understanding of the human world was usually a little befuddled at the best of times. She did not fully understand the human language like Hazel did. She only caught certain words which were repeated often, as was the case now.

"What's a *letta*?" asked Alfie.

Too late – Madam had gone back to sleep (or rather she pretended to, as she didn't actually know what a 'letta' was).

Hazel gave Alfie a quick explanation of how such things carried information between humans, before asking Madam if she knew anything about its contents. The deathly silence coming from the Pomeranian suggested she did not. For now, that mystery would have to wait

Hazel now inquired after Molly. According to Skip, she was spending more and more time cooped up in her room. She was frequently sad and often in tears. It seemed to involve the object she carried with her at all times.

"That's a mobile foam," said Madam Pom with authority, although her eyes were still shut. Had they been open, she would have looked at the others in disgust for not knowing this basic fact from the human world. She offered no more information than this, for that was all she knew.

Hazel made no attempt to tell her the word was actually 'phone' as arguing with Madam Pom was never an idea worth considering. She had noticed herself how much Molly focused on her phone, even at breakfast time in the kitchen. What was making her so sad? That would take some investigating.

For now, she looked out at the sky through the window of the outhouse. The Full Moon was casting her bright silver light through the darkness. That meant The Moon Queen would be back.

The animals of the house always looked forward to seeing her. That even included Madam Pom, who had had to be taught such a sharp lesson by the monarch after her initial treatment of the guinea pigs. Fortunately, all was now forgiven and forgotten.

The monthly meeting with the Moon Queen was always an event worth waiting for. Although the sprites: Godfrig, Merriel, Oro and Fion, were available any evening should the guinea pigs truly need them, the meeting with the monarch was special. Delicious wild plants and herbs, provided by Godfrig, would be enjoyed by the light of Fion's fiery torches and the gentle music of Oro's reed pipe. They would be washed down by the purest crystal clear water from Merriel's clamshell. The Queen would listen to the latest news from the garden, although Hazel always felt the monarch was well aware of all events within her kingdom.

At last, nightfall came. Mr Greenwood had come inside and taken himself off to bed, so the coast was clear for the animals to go out into the garden.

The guinea pigs slipped out through the hole in the wall and squeezed their way behind the camellia bush, whilst

Skip and Madam Pom went out through the dog flap in the kitchen door to join them.

Together, Hazel, Alfie, Piggy Mama, Little Rufus, Skip and Madam Pom made their way down the lawn to the bottom of the garden where the silver birch tree stood. By its elegant silver trunk, the figures of The Moon Queen and her sprites could be seen, already transformed from their daytime appearances of stone.

The animals stopped a little distance away, respectfully waiting to be invited forwards by the monarch.

The Moon Queen's face was as serene and expressionless as ever, but the moonstone atop of the staff in her hand glowed with the pleasure she felt at seeing Hazel and the others.

"Come forward, little ones," she said gently, "We have been expecting you."

Once settled, the Queen asked how they had been since her last visit and enquired after their latest news.

As they ate the delicious delicacies served up by Godfrig, Hazel told Her Majesty about the sadness in the Greenwood home. She described Billy's frequent bursts of anger and Molly's continual sadness.

The Moon Queen listened and said, "It is to be expected. The young ones will be missing their mother. The anniversary of her loss approaches soon."

Merriel spoke next, "We used to love seeing her in the garden with her children. She was so warm and caring, both to them and all the creatures who visited."

"If only her family realised how close she still is," said Godfrig softly.

"Humans see so little!" said Fion sharply. "They don't even see what's in front of their noses!"

The Moon Queen smiled at her fiery sprite. "Certainly, they could know more, Fion, if they were able to open their eyes to all the possibilities in the universe. But they do not know how, so we must forgive them"

As if to underline this fact, Oro began to play a gentle tune upon his reed pipe, catching the mood of the party.

Once the evening had finished, and the time came to depart, The Moon Queen asked Hazel to wait as her family and the Pomeranians made their way back up the garden, accompanied by the sprites as orbs, lighting the way.

"Hazel," she began, "I know you often have many plans

in life. I have given you a new gift which may help in what you do. When the time is right, it will show itself."

Hazel had to swallow the desperate urge to ask what it might be. She merely thanked the monarch for her continuing kindness with a grateful smile.

The Moon Queen returned the smile. "We will meet again when My Lady in the Sky is at her fullest once more. In the meantime, remember my sprites are here for you, when needed. Use them sparingly and wisely. Now go with my blessing."

Hazel thanked The Moon Queen once more and bade her goodnight, before wandering back up the lawn, accompanied by the sprites.

As she took her leave of them, questions crowded her mind. What was going on with the Greenwood family? What could she do to help? And what new gift had the Moon Queen given her?

Chapter 5
The Letter

HAZEL could not sleep. She was unable to clear her mind of all the worries and excitement of the day. Something was troubling Billy and Molly, and Hazel wanted to know more.

The Greenwoods had provided her and her family with all the love and care they could ever need, and a home they could only ever have dreamt of. It was now time to repay that kindness.

Without waking the other piggies, she left the hutch and soon found Skip in the kitchen on his comfy bed, his chew toy beneath his paw. He was always alert, and soon awoke at the sound of Hazel's feet on the floor.

Madam Pom, on the other hand, was sound asleep, snoring as loudly as ever.

"Skip," whispered Hazel, "I need to find out more about what's going on with Billy and Molly. Will you help me get upstairs to the bedrooms?"

"Okay!" replied Skip, always happy to please.

The steep, winding staircase in the old Georgian house was not an easy climb for a guinea pig, even one as determined as Hazel. So, she had to clamber on board Skip's back, as she had done previously, and hold on tightly to his long fur.

After much effort, they both finally reached the landing at the top. The first door they reached was firmly shut. This, Hazel recognised as Molly's room, from the occasions when she had been taken upstairs. She pushed a paw against the sturdy old wooden door, but there was no sign of any give.

She gave a deep sigh of frustration. There was no obvious way to access her room, so that part of the night's investigations would have to wait to another time.

Regretfully, Hazel turned her attentions to the doorway opposite. This, Hazel knew belonged to Billy. The door stood slightly ajar.

The gap between door and frame was wide enough for Hazel to slip through. Skip quietly used all his strength to nudge the door open some more, so he could follow Hazel in.

As Billy never shut his curtains, the light of the moon lit the room enough for Hazel to see quite well. There on the floor was a ball of screwed up paper. She wondered if that was the letter which caused all the night's arguments. She tentatively reached out a paw to take hold of it and look for clues.

As quietly as she could, Hazel pulled at the paper. In the still of the night, the noise seemed magnified many times over. Her heart thumped as Billy stirred in his sleep and turned over. Fortunately, he was a heavy sleeper and did not awake.

As Hazel unfolded what was indeed the letter, she could see the ink marks which she knew humans could look at and understand.

With it now smoothed out, Hazel recognised the school emblem from Billy's exercise books. It was of an oak tree with brambles around its roots. At the top it had the heading, *Brierley Bramble Junior School.* Beneath it said:

Dear Mr Greenwood. With regard to your son, Billy … Hazel stopped, frozen in shock.

How did she know what it said? She looked again – the ink marks now actually meant something to her. The guinea pig blinked in disbelief. Her paws trembled and she swallowed hard, her heart thumping.

A further examination of the letter brought the same conclusion. "Skip!" she announced in an excited whisper, "I think I can *read!*"

Hazel could barely contain her excitement. This had to be the new gift promised by The Moon Queen. She never failed to surprise the guinea pig with her kindness and generosity. It would open up a world of possibilities for her.

Skip licked Hazel's ear to congratulate her, and wagged his tail cheerfully.

The guinea pig glanced around the room to check she was not imagining things. Sure enough, by the light of the moon, she could read the posters on Billy's walls: *Butterflies of the UK ... British Garden Birds ... Planets of Our Solar System...*

Not all words made sense to her, but she could read what they said.

Hazel wasted no more time, she needed to know what this letter was all about. It seemed to be a list of complaints about Billy's conduct at school:

Awkward during Mother's Day assembly ... wouldn't sit still for literacy ... told Miss Robinson that he couldn't care less about fronted adverbials or expanded noun phrases... grabbed another pupil for stamping on a worm ... climbed over the school fence at breaktime to escape fractions again ...

Hazel could not understand every part, but she understood the main ideas. She sighed deeply. Poor Billy. No wonder he was angry.

Meeting with the governors arranged ... committee headed by our new Chair of Governors, Mrs Hortense Pepper.

Hazel stopped at the name *Mrs Pepper.* Wasn't that the woman who had moved into the cottage next door to Betty?

She carried on reading: *Low data scores ... failing to meet targets ... school's position in league tables ... reputation in the local community ...*

Again, such phrases meant little to the guinea pig, however, she could guess that none of it was positive from the general tone of the letter.

Hazel was most curious about this Mrs Pepper. How was her name already appearing on a letter from Billy's school?

That question would be answered all too soon.

Chapter 6
The New Chair of Governors

As the warm light filtered through the blinds in the windows of Brierley Bramble Junior School, Mrs Kinder the headmistress was sitting in her office doing her best to remain calm.

This was proving rather difficult, for sitting opposite her, was the new Chair of Governors, Mrs Hortense Pepper. The lady herself had been in the position for a relatively short time, but it seemed like forever to those around her. She had been able to take up the position simply because no one else had time to do the job at present.

Mrs Kinder wondered if Mrs Pepper actually liked her own home, as she never seemed to be in it. Instead, she was forever prowling around the school on a mission to 'check standards'.

Each visit brought a fresh bout of criticism: Was enough homework being set? Why were children no longer expected to recite their times tables? What about learning poetry off by heart? Surely art afternoon was a waste of time when they could squeeze in more literacy ...

It took every bit of self-control the headmistress

possessed to restrain her feelings, as she swallowed the latest opinions from the Chair of Governors.

"Mrs Pepper," she said icily, "a governor is supposed to be a critical friend. All I seem to hear is the critical bit."

Mrs Pepper glared at Mrs Kinder over half-moon spectacles, as she replied smoothly, "Mrs Kinder, a good friend will tell you the truth, even if it hurts."

The headmistress tried breathing deeply to contain her rising anger and irritation before retorting, "Well, Mrs Pepper, forgive me if I consider it *my* job to run the school – I am, after all, the headteacher."

The response was swift and cool from Mrs Pepper who responded, "May I remind you, Mrs Kinder, that I too am responsible for ensuring the school meets certain academic standards."

On her lap, she had the latest data sheets, tightly clasped together in a black bulldog clip. The Chair of Governors had been making it clear that she was most unhappy with the information they revealed.

Mrs Kinder had come to dread Mrs Pepper's visits and her sheets of facts and figures.

To the headmistress, each child was like a flower grown from seed. No two young shoots were exactly alike; each had their own special qualities, and their own talents and skills. She firmly believed that education was about nurturing each youngster as they blossomed in their own unique ways.

How she disliked the cold, harsh, simplistic data that now categorised each child. It felt so unnatural to rank their progress in any subject on the curriculum within a single figure, and then impose targets for their future from a computer algorithm. She had made the decision to retire early some time ago, and the new ways of education had certainly helped with that decision.

Mrs Pepper had no such finer feelings. Like an accountant, she loved facts and figures, nicely lined up in columns, with everything in good order – the same as her clothes: neat, tidy and smart.

She insisted on everything being in paper form, the old fashioned way. "You know I never touch computers or any of that new-fangled modern technology," she would always remind Mrs Kinder in a smooth, steely voice whenever the subject was raised.

Mrs Pepper clutched her data sheets ever tighter in her hands as she announced, "Mrs Kinder, the time has come for us to take action. We need to conduct interviews with the parents of the children who are letting us down and failing to achieve what they should."

"Letting us down?" replied Mrs Kinder, aghast.

"Indeed," said Mrs Pepper indignantly, "our place in the local league tables is in danger of slipping. Do you want the local education authority breathing down our necks, Mrs Kinder?"

Mrs Kinder resisted the urge to throttle Mrs Pepper with the necktie of her own silk blouse, by repeating the words 'retiring soon' in her head over and over again, until she could speak with a calm voice.

"You must do as you see fit, Mrs Pepper. I'm sure you will anyway. Now if you'll excuse me," she said, standing to leave, "I promised the year six pupils that we would check on the progress of our school allotment before break."

Mrs Pepper tried to keep the scorn from her voice at hearing of this complete waste of valuable school time. Curtly, she bid the headmistress good day, before bustling from the office, and sweeping out of the school building with her precious sheets of data lodged securely in her voluminous black handbag.

There was really no need to drive the short distance from her home to Brierley Bramble Junior School, but Mrs Pepper liked to do so.

As she stepped into her car and sat in the driver's seat, she took a quick glance around to ensure no one was looking. The Chair of Governors then opened her large handbag and removed a slim silver smartphone from its depths. She pressed the screen and began to tap the keys.

Chapter 7
The Magpies

On the edge of the village of Brierley Bramble, the grounds of the old estate provided an unspoilt haven for wildlife and humans alike. The green space stretched as far as the eye could see until it met Lundy Woods in the distance. Once upon a time, the grand old home of the local squire had stood there, until the war years came, when it was requisitioned for military use. Local mining work destabilised the foundations, leaving the house unsafe enough to be demolished. Now the mere outline of where it once stood was all that remained of its wonderful grandeur.

Hazel would often visit there with Blake. Many a time she wondered what tales the walls of that old house could have told, and what memories they once held.

On this calm, clear morning of bright blue skies, the guinea pig was on her way there once more, nestled in the warm grey and white feathers of the faithful bird's back.

It had been a place to avoid for the past few days. A music festival had taken place in its spacious grounds. Deep bass notes and lively rhythms, loud voices and bright flashing lights had punctured the quiet of the countryside. Explosive fireworks had added to the general cacophony.

The thunderous sounds had alarmed and unsettled the wildlife and disturbed the residents of the surrounding villages, but now it had finally ended. Peace and tranquillity had returned.

Or so Hazel and Blake thought.

Upon arrival, the guinea pig and the heron stared in disbelief. Where once there had been a peaceful green space, there now was an ocean of human debris: abandoned tents, takeaway wrappers and plastic carrier bags sitting alongside bottles, cans, crisp packets and general rubbish, smothering the grass in a sea of waste. The burning embers of a camp fire still glowed amongst a pile of stones, surrounded by scorch marks in the grass.

The local wildlife was out in force scavenging what it could from the waste. Birds, squirrels, foxes and the odd badger were busily investigating the left- behind wrappers and scraps of food. Bruce the tomcat, and a few of his pals, could be seen searching for tasty morsels to supplement their daily diet too.

It took some time before Hazel and Blake could each process what they saw, and put any thoughts into words.

Hazel looked up at Blake in disbelief. "Why have the humans done this, Blake?"

The heron looked back at Hazel with sorrowful eyes and replied, "I really don't know."

The answer was actually quite simple. One couple had packed up and left behind their cheap disposable tent, along with any other items they did not care to carry. Then, their neighbours had done the same. Each individual thought their small mess didn't matter. They had had their fun now, and they were off back home, travelling light without a care in the world.

So, within twenty four hours, nature was left under siege by a huge collection of small messes, together which formed a gigantic mess of horrifying proportions.

As Hazel and Blake gazed at the sight before them, Hazel shuddered with horror. There were opened food tins with sharp edges, tempting for small animals to creep inside and lick the contents; broken glass to cut small feet, and delicate paws; plastic bags and sheeting to trap and suffocate ... All manner of terrible traps lay around.

The guinea pig and the heron soon became aware of creatures in real trouble: a hedgehog wedged in a glass jar, a slow worm trapped in a bottle and a pigeon with a cord wound tightly around its leg.

Hazel freed the bird by putting her gnawing skills to use. One very grateful pigeon thanked her and hastily took its leave. Blake freed the other two victims by tapping hard on the glass each time with a stone in his beak, until it gave way. The hedgehog scampered free, calling back her gratitude over her shoulder. The slow worm, however, was in a complete panic and scuttled off without his tail. "Don't worry," Blake reassured a dismayed Hazel. "A slow worm's tail always grows back again."

A few more rescues later, they were both exhausted, but their biggest challenge was still to come.

From beneath the layers of a plastic tent, cries of panic could be heard.

Blake held his head to one side and listened intently. "I hear young rabbits," he said. "It sounds like they're in there with their mother."

Hazel looked at the tent in horror. The poor little things. There was a large, nibbled hole in the top of the tent material where the animals had clearly made their way in, no doubt sensing food, but they were now trapped in the layers of the fabric.

Hazel tried to poke her nose beneath the rim of the tent, but this one had a heavy metal frame which was beyond her strength.

Blake tried too, but to no avail. The cries were getting louder, and the mother rabbit was now joining in. The guinea pig and the heron began to despair, until they heard a voice behind them,

"Can I assist?" it asked.

A young magpie was looking down at them from a tree. "I know you, don't I?" he asked, looking at Hazel.

She looked back puzzled.

"You live at the big house at the edge of the village, don't you? The one surrounded by meadows," the bird continued.

"Yes," said Hazel still baffled.

"I was helped there once," said the magpie. "I was injured in the fields and couldn't fly – a boy picked me up from under the hedgerow. He took me to that house, and I was nursed back to health."

He continued, "I've seen you in the garden since. I often go there with my friends as we birds like the pleasant atmosphere."

He hopped down. "The name's Magus," he said. "So, what's the problem?"

He seemed genuinely interested or at least curious, so Hazel introduced Blake, and then explained the situation. She felt slightly afraid, but the baby rabbits' calls were becoming ever more urgent, and she remembered Mama telling her how clever magpies were. Magus could well be their last hope if those young creatures were not to die of fright, as rabbits were so prone to do.

"The rim's too heavy for us," she explained.

Magus hopped around the collapsed tent, pecking at the rim to test its weight. His keen bird brain was thinking things through.

"Back in a moment," he announced before flying off into the air.

He was soon back with a long piece of metal wire in his mouth. He put his foot on one end and, at the other, he used his beak to fashion a hook.

The magpie placed the hook under the rim of the tent and grabbed the straight end in his foot. He then attempted to fly upwards. The rim rose a little, but the weight was too much and soon flopped back down.

"I think," said Magus, "we need further help."

With that, he flapped his wings and was gone in an instant. Hazel and Blake watched him disappear off into the sky. Sometime later, he returned with a whole gulp of magpies.

They each had metal hooks held in their mouths. Blake knew enough about the world to recognise that some were formed from car aerials, some from wire coat hangers and the rest from bits of fencing.

Magus had given up his hook to another bird and was now coordinating the rescue efforts. Each magpie got itself in position around the rim of the tent with its hook in its beak, and slipped it beneath the metal. It was clear that they were going to fly in formation and lift up the tent together. Mama had been right about the intelligence of magpies.

As this crossed Hazel's mind, it was very quickly followed by a thought which chilled her blood. Mama had told her something else about magpies – they enjoyed baby rabbits for dinner.

Hazel gasped in horror. Had Magus just tricked them? Was it all simply a plan to get a meal for himself and his friends?

Hazel tried to cry out – but too late. The magpies, as one, rose up into the air, their wings flapping hard with the weight of the tent.

As the tent rose higher, the baby rabbits and their mother dashed for their lives from beneath its material. Once the rabbit family had gained their freedom, the magpies dropped the tent and began to give chase.

It all seemed to happen in slow motion. Hazel and Blake froze in dread. Had they just helped the baby rabbits to die?

At that very moment, there was a volley of loud shots.

It was now the magpies who feared for their lives. They were well used to the sound of guns and knew what it meant for them. They stopped their pursuit in mid-air and pointed their faces upwards, flapping with all their might to get as far away as possible.

By now, the rabbit family had gone too, safely hidden away somewhere, far from the eyes of predators.

Hazel and Blake had dived for cover beneath the nearest tree. Both were trembling with fright when Magus reappeared beside them.

"You're quite safe!" he announced happily.

Hazel and Blake stared at him, still too shocked to speak.

Hazel eventually found her voice, and it was angry. "You wanted to eat those baby rabbits, didn't you?!" she shouted furiously. "If those guns hadn't fired …"

Magus laughed, "There were no guns!"

He cheerfully continued, "I found some firecrackers in amongst the rubbish and dropped them in that campfire over there. I just had to get my timing right."

With that, he winked at Hazel and Blake, and began to flap his wings. "Just don't tell my friends!" he called as he made his way off into the sky. "See you around!"

The guinea pig and the heron looked at each other and dissolved into laughter, more from relief than mirth. What a strange afternoon.

Thankfully, at this point, they could see no more animals in distress. Yet, the longer the rubbish stayed here, the more chance there was of further animals becoming trapped, injured or worse ...

What on earth could they do? The humans had made this mess and they were the only ones who could shift it.

At that moment, as if their prayers had been answered, the noise of many, many human voices sounded in the air.

Chapter 8
A Stroll Through the Park

IT was PC Frankie, cycling along on one of his early morning rides, who had spotted the awful scene of devastation left behind by the festival. He had pedalled at top speed to raise the alarm with his fellow residents of Brierley Bramble.

His first port of call had been the Greenwoods' house, where he knew John would be in his workshop that day.

Other villagers had heeded the call immediately and had taken or begged the day off work to deal with this local emergency. They were now arriving, armed with large refuse sacks, litter grabbers and thick gloves, each ready to do their bit and clear up the mess.

On this pleasant morning of sunshine, the atmosphere was cheerful and full of team spirit. Whole families strolled along, young and old, side by side. Grandmas and grandads walked alongside parents with toddlers in bright tee shirts, babies in prams and dogs on leads.

Mrs Kinder had stopped all lessons for the day, and organised her pupils into an army of young helpers, eager and keen to make a difference and show they cared.

All her young charges were safely recognisable in their bright orange and yellow team bibs, borrowed from the P.E.

cupboard. Many had been joined by their parents, whilst those who weren't were firmly under the careful supervision of their teachers.

The Greenwoods, with Madam Pom and Skip, led the crowd of helpers. Billy, Molly and their father each wore hi vis orange tabards, plus a look of determination on their faces.

Behind them, walked Betty Albright, PC Frankie and his wife, farmer Jack Lewis, Constance Clark the vet and Neville Frost the paramedic, amongst numerous others. Ernie Bostock followed at the rear with other shopkeepers. Without a second thought, they had shut up shop for the day to come and do their bit, carried along by outrage at the damage done to their community.

Hazel and Blake had taken up position on the top of a large beech tree, giving themselves a prime position to watch all events below.

The guinea pig's heart swelled with pride at the sight of the Greenwoods leading the way.

Sadly, her joy was short lived.

"Everybody stop!" cried a shrill voice.

All present turned to see Mrs Pepper looking outraged, with a megaphone in one hand, and a clipboard clasped tightly in the other.

"Who is in charge of this?" she demanded. "Well?" Mrs Pepper asked once more, glaring fiercely at John Greenwood, with suspicion in her eyes.

"I am happy to speak on behalf of everyone here, Mrs Pepper," replied Mr Greenwood calmly.

"I see," she responded sharply.

Mrs Pepper peered at John over her half-moon spectacles, and asked in a voice laced with ill-concealed fury, "Have you filled in the appropriate paperwork for this event?"

Mr Greenwood raised his eyebrows and tried to speak, but was given little chance. Mrs Pepper was sensing victory.

She carried on, "You must know that the local council insist on public liability insurance for an organised event like this, plus a full and proper risk assessment."

"Mrs Pepper ..." began Mr Greenwood.

"*Mr Greenwood,*" she interrupted. "This event simply cannot go ahead without the relevant paperwork! I have been to the council headquarters this very morning and spoken to the council leader himself."

She triumphantly produced her clipboard, to which was attached an official- looking document. She now brandished this beneath the nose of Mr Greenwood.

He took the document from Mrs Pepper and glanced over it. PC Frankie stepped forward. "May I take a look at that, John?"

After looking closely at it, the police officer sadly shook his head and agreed it was correct.

"Okay," said Mr Greenwood quietly and heavily, "you win, Mrs Pepper. The law is clearly on your side."

To the surprise of everyone present (except Mrs Pepper) Mr Greenwood slowly removed his hi vis tabard and folded it neatly, before placing it inside his backpack.

Billy stared in disbelief. How could his dad let him down like this? The other Brierley Bramble residents stared too. An air of desolation descended over the crowd, replacing the party atmosphere of moments before. The people of Brierley Bramble had always had a healthy disregard for official rules, and had certainly expected John Greenwood, of all people, to put up more of a fight.

From where she listened, Hazel's heart sank. So, this was Mrs Pepper. Not only had she made trouble for Billy, but she was now also upsetting the whole village. She had even got the better of Mr Greenwood.

Betty started to speak, "John..."

Mr Greenwood looked at her with heavy eyes and sighed. "It's no use, Betty. Mrs Pepper has officialdom on her side. We cannot break the law."

Billy hid his face. His lips trembled and angry tears stung his eyes. Molly put a protective arm around him and glared at her father.

"Billy, Molly, take your tabards off too," he said in the quiet, steely voice that they both knew was not to be argued with.

Mr Greenwood turned his gaze towards the assembled villagers. "We have to remove the bibs everybody or we will indeed be in trouble."

Mrs Pepper watched with undisguised pleasure at her day's work. The villagers would think twice in future before doing such things without consulting her.

All around removed their orange bibs and tabards and packed them away. A few families turned, ready to leave the park, and disappointed children began to cry.

Mr Greenwood began to speak loudly, enough for those at the back to hear. "Well, now that the official event is off, I'm going on a nice stroll through the grounds of the estate with my two children."

He looked pointedly at Billy and Molly. "Remember, you two, that we need as many different coloured glass bottles as you can find for that art project Molly has for the summer holiday."

His two children looked back with puzzled faces.

"Betty," he continued in a loud voice, "Didn't you tell me you needed plastic bags to line the bottom of your plant containers?"

Betty smiled back with a knowing grin, "Indeed I do, John," she answered at top volume. "I might just go for a stroll myself and see if I can find any!"

"Jim," continued Mr Greenwood as loudly as ever, "are you still making kites these days for the grandkids? I believe tent material is good for that."

"Oh yes," yelled P.C. Frankie cheerfully. "Do you know, I was just thinking about that. My good lady wife and I might see if we come across any on our walk. If anyone else could help, I'd be grateful!"

At this, Neville Frost, the paramedic and keen gardener, declared, "I wonder if there might be any crisp packets blowing about on the breeze today. I really need some for keeping all my dried seeds in, come the autumn. Could any children assist me please?"

Constance Clark, the local vet, was the next to chip in vociferously, "I need plastic bottles to fill with water and freeze. They make great water coolers for the animals back at the surgery. Could anyone help me find some?"

Others soon got the message and announced their need to find beer cans, takeaway wrappers and other sundry items – all for their own personal use, of course, and only as they happened to enjoy a walk in the park.

By now, Mrs Pepper was almost purple with indignation. She turned her attention to Mrs Kinder, pronouncing her words with dangerous icy calm. "Do please explain to me, Mrs Kinder, why these children are not in school."

The headteacher smiled like The Mona Lisa, and replied, "Why, Mrs Pepper it's all part of a new Woodland Schools initiative. I've been meaning to mention it to you. I've had the official paperwork ready for some time. It was agreed with our previous Chair of Governors. We have a copy of the policy available on the school website. If only you had access to a computer," she said wryly.

The headteacher turned to go, before adding warmly, "Do feel free to join us, Mrs Pepper. I'm sure you would find it most educational."

With a grin of sheer delight, Mrs Kinder led her children onwards for a spell in the sunshine, searching for art materials on the theme of 'recycling'.

The Chair of Governors sighed deeply. There were no more words to be said. The megaphone drooped in her hand, and the clipboard hung loosely by her side. She stood like a forlorn statue, as Mrs Kinder and her children, along with all the other residents of Brierley Bramble, resumed their day out in the park.

Hazel and Blake had seen enough. The cheery atmosphere of the human gathering was quite infectious. They made their way home, freewheeling contentedly through the sky, happy in the knowledge that the estate would soon be back to its former glory.

Chapter 9
Bring Your Pet to School

THERE was a spring in the step of Mrs Kinder as she walked through the doors of Brierley Bramble Junior School that morning. She had just had one of her bright ideas during the stroll to work, and was now working out the details in her head.

Show and Tell had become a little stale recently. The usual invitation for children to talk about any interesting experience they had had, or object they had acquired, had become limited to small erasers with faces on, play fights by the boys, or rather long, rambling accounts from children who lost the interest of those listening with excessive details.

So, Mrs Kinder decided to introduce *Bring Your Small Pet to School* as an alternative. This new idea would involve children putting their names on slips of paper in a box, from which one slip would be randomly selected. It would then be that child's turn to bring in any small pet which could be transported in some sort of container, like a hamster, gerbil, tortoise, guinea pig or similar.

There was an ulterior motive for this brainwave. Fridays were becoming a real problem where Billy Greenwood was concerned. It was the day when English grammar was the focus of Literacy Hour, and so was the day when he was most likely to make another escape attempt from school during break time.

Animals were such a passion of his that it might just encourage him to stay put, especially if the animals were his. Of course, the fact that it would irritate Mrs Pepper was simply an additional bonus.

The headmistress had a plan in place by the time she sat down in her office.

Later that day, once the children had been registered, and numbers collected for who was having sandwiches or school lunch that day, Mrs Kinder entered Billy's classroom, with a cardboard box in one hand, and small slips of paper in the other.

Upon hearing what it was for, many children excitedly put their hands up for a slip to write their name on. Once all had filled them in, Mrs Kinder walked around the desks with the box, allowing pupils to post their pieces of paper.

Returning to the front of the classroom, she opened the box and stirred the contents with her hand. As the children waited with bated breath, she pretended to pull one out, producing instead the slip she had held in her hand all along.

And so it was that Billy Greenwood had the honour of being the very first child selected to bring in his precious pets. He announced to the class, in a proud voice, that he would be bringing in his four guinea pigs the very next day.

Chapter 10
The School Visit

FOR once, Billy was actually looking forward to going to school. Hazel, Alfie, Piggy Mama and Little Rufus had each had a nail trim and been brushed to look their best. They were now sitting expectantly in their carry cage, ready for their visit to Brierley Bramble Juniors.

Hazel had overheard Billy discussing the visit with his father, and had explained it all to the rest of her family. They were still a little apprehensive, especially Little Rufus, who was more than unhappy at leaving the security of the outhouse. However, once Billy had supplied a nice pile of fresh green grass, the youngest piggy forgot all about his nerves, and busied himself with trying to eat more than Alfie.

The nerves did return once they were loaded into Mr Greenwood's truck, but the journey on Billy's lap took only a short time. Next thing they knew, the engine stopped, and they were being carried through the fresh air, into school reception, down the corridor and finally into Billy's classroom. The cage came to rest on a desk at the front of the room.

The four piggies waited expectantly. Strange sounds and

smells surrounded them as they waited. So, this was the place Billy went off to each weekday.

There was no time for any more thoughts, for the door now opened and the class of children poured in. They soon spotted the guinea pigs. Curious faces surrounded the cage, with a few small fingers being poked through and offered to the guinea pigs inside.

The piggies huddled close and did their best to avoid contact with any of the fingers.

"I do like the pretty brown and white one," said Ella Paterson gently, as she looked into the cage.

"Aw, look at the little white one with a patch over his eye!" exclaimed Gemma Peacock, rather less gently.

"I like the one with a tuft on his head – he's cute!" announced Tommy Taylor, as he waggled his fingers through the bars.

"That one's boring – it's all brown!" declared Louise Little, much to Billy's annoyance.

Fortunately, that last insulting comment was lost on its

recipient, Piggy Mama, as she could not understand much of the human language.

Eventually, the children were all shooed away by the teacher and told to take their seats. Once the register had been taken, Billy was given a ten minute slot to introduce his pets to the class and answer any questions on them. Mrs Kinder popped in to listen, and gave Billy a warm smile when the session ended. He had beamed with pride whilst talking about his beloved guinea pigs.

The cage was now moved to a table at the back of the class near Billy's desk.

It was time for numeracy. Alfie and Little Rufus yawned and went to sleep, whilst Mama tried to stay awake, but found her eyes closing too. In contrast, Hazel listened closely. Her ability to understand the language meant she was learning alongside the children, and she found it fascinating. She worked out the answers to questions long before the pupils in the class. The small guinea pig was quite disappointed when breaktime came.

When the children filed back in after break, chaos reigned for a time. One group of boys had had a punch up over a football game on the playground. Four of them had to be given wet paper towels to hold over cuts and bruises as they sat at their desks. Two sets of girls had fallen out and were now crying, whilst three further children had headaches. They too were given wet paper towels by an increasingly exasperated Miss Robinson.

Calm was finally restored, and the young teacher began her literacy lesson. It was the one on grammar, which Mrs Kinder had predicted would be a problem. Billy's head was soon down on the desk. He gave up at the sound of the word *clause.*

After the explanatory part, the children were given worksheets to fill in, in order to demonstrate the new knowledge they had acquired – or as in Billy's case – had not.

The lesson was interrupted by the arrival of Mrs Pepper. The Chair of Governors had come to see how the lesson was going. She had heard it was to be on grammar - a subject of which she fully approved.

The young pupils had become very used to seeing her around the school. They did not fully understand who she was, but knew she was somebody important, so always put on their best behaviour whenever she appeared in the room.

Mrs Pepper began to patrol the desks, looking over the shoulder of each child as they worked, pointing out any errors with a polished finger nail. Miss Robinson tried her best to look unconcerned as she assisted a queue of children at her desk, asking for spellings.

Hazel feared the worst. It would not be long before the Chair of Governors arrived at Billy's desk. She could see his worksheet was rather bare compared to the other children's. He had tried the first three questions, then had become bored and so began drawing a picture of a guinea pig on the sheet, instead.

Louise Little had noticed. Her hand shot into the air. "Miss Robinson, Billy Greenwood's not doing any work!"

"Yeah," added her best friend, Gemma Peacock. "He's got his head on the desk again!"

Everyone stopped to look at Billy, including Mrs Pepper.

Hazel could see his temper starting to rise. He had already gone red, partly with embarrassment, and partly with anger at the two girls. If he reacted badly here, he could be in terrible trouble. He was already in Mrs Pepper's bad books

Hazel knew she had to create a distraction. She wracked her brains and did the only thing she could think of. She stood up on her back legs, threw back her head and began to sing, just as she once had in the garden of Bowood, after her first meeting with The Moon Queen.

Alfie, Mama and Little Rufus stared at her in amazement. They were unaware she could do such a thing. However, their surprise could not compare to that of the children in the class.

Complete silence descended on the classroom. Everyone stared at the cage of guinea pigs. Next came the reaction as children squealed and pointed at the cage.

"Miss, Miss! The guinea pig just made a funny noise!"

"Miss, that guinea pig was chirping like a bird!"

"It was singing, Miss!"

Some children leapt from their seats and began crowding round the cage.

"Children!" shouted Miss Robinson. "Get back to your seats immediately!"

The chaos had the desired effect. Mrs Pepper had lost interest in Billy and was staring at Hazel. Her stare was so intense, that it made the guinea pig feel rather uncomfortable.

Thankfully, the headmistress, Mrs Kinder, arrived at this point, wanting to know what all the commotion was about.

When she heard the explanation,

she said cheerfully, "Perhaps we should look online and see if guinea pigs can indeed sing, Miss Robinson. What do you think, children?"

The pupils chorused their approval.

"If you'll excuse me," said the Chair of Governors icily, "I will leave you to it, Mrs Kinder. You know technology is not my preferred source of information. I'd rather look it up in a proper reference book. You can trust those more."

On that note, she turned around and left the room, staring hard once more at Hazel.

Mrs Kinder rolled her eyes at Miss Robinson, whispering, "She won't even touch a mobile phone!"

The young teacher looked back in amazement, "Really? In this day and age?"

"Miss Robinson," interrupted Louise Little with her hand in the air, "It's lunchtime!"

"Okay," replied the teacher. "We'll leave it there, children. Wash your hands and get lined up."

The children obeyed instantly. It was chips for lunch on Fridays, and they didn't need telling twice. Billy, normally first in the queue, took his time today and gave the piggies a quick stroke through the bars before going off to wash his hands.

Lunchboxes were collected from the special trolley, and children took their seats in the dining hall, or queued up at the food counter.

In the quiet of the now empty classroom, the guinea pig family discussed the events of the morning. Today was the first time that Alfie, Mama and Little Rufus had set eyes on the famous Mrs Pepper. They each agreed she was a very frightening person.

"I think we need to know more about her," announced Hazel. "This might be the perfect chance."

Before Mama had time to protest, Hazel undid the simple catch on the door of the cage, and jumped out onto Billy's desk. From there it was a small jump onto his chair, which he had not bothered to push under, and a slightly longer one onto the carpeted floor.

She was joined by Alfie, close behind her.

"For goodness sake, be careful!" called Mama, resigned to the fact that she could not now stop her two headstrong young ones. Little Rufus would have followed too had she not put her foot down.

"Where shall we go?" Alfie asked.

"This way," replied Hazel, "I can smell her perfume."

The two piggies scampered along the corridor, following the scent of Mrs Pepper, keeping close to the wall. They passed reception where the school secretary was too focused on her tasty lunch of tuna sandwich and hand-cooked sweet chilli crisps to notice them.

They stopped as they got to the open door of Mrs Kinder's office. The two guinea pigs could see Mrs Pepper inside. She was looking rather furtive.

There was just enough room for Hazel and Alfie to squeeze through the gap, without disturbing the door, so they did just that. A padded chair provided the perfect cover to hide beneath.

The two guinea pigs watched in amazement as they saw Mrs Pepper reach down into a large black handbag and take out a silver smartphone. She sat down and began to tap away on it, her fingers moving across the keypad with ease. Hazel and Alfie exchanged glances. They had just heard her claim to hate all technology!

So why, they wondered, did Mrs Pepper have a secret mobile phone?

Chapter 11
Molly's Secret

It had all been going so well for Molly Greenwood over the past term at school. She had a new friend, a girl named Priscilla, who had arrived at *Morecaston High School* earlier in the year.

Molly had had other friends at school, but no one close. The constant fall outs with girls, often motivated by petty jealousies, wore her down. They had become an annoying part of everyday life. Girls, it seemed, could simply not be friends without complications.

Priscilla had been equally bruised by other girls' fickle natures. She too had lost out in the popularity stakes, and was happy to find a good friend in Molly.

The friendship had originally begun through their mutual love of art. They sat next to each other in art lessons, and both attended the after school art club together on Fridays. As Priscilla lived in Morecaston, they communicated the rest of the time on social media.

When the annual competition for the best Carnival Day poster was announced in Brierley Bramble, Molly couldn't wait to tell Priscilla. Together, the girls prepared their entries, sharing ideas, suggesting improvements, and sent them in on the same day, waiting with their fingers crossed.

To her total disbelief, Molly was awarded the top prize, and Priscilla came runner up. The two friends were overjoyed.

A photograph duly appeared in the local newspaper, *The Morecaston Times,* with the caption: *Molly Greenwood and Priscilla Montague, proud winners of this year's Brierley Bramble carnival poster competition.* It was replicated on social media.

That was when it all began.

Beneath the covers of her bed, Molly wept, and not for the first time. She could not take her eyes off the screen on her phone. She was on the social media app *AskMe,* yet again. She had to look. She couldn't resist. She needed to know what they were saying this time.

The app was intended for teenage girls to ask questions and offer opinions on music, films, cosmetics and anything else of interest. All posts were anonymous, so girls could contribute with confidence, without anyone knowing their identity.

However, the platform had now become used in a rather different way from that originally intended. The young, inventive as ever, had subverted it for a different purpose – to gossip and mock others.

A new discussion thread had appeared, entitled, *CarrotTopMollyGreenwood.* It was becoming ever more popular by the day. It had begun with a simple question:

Who knew carrot tops could win prizes?

That truly hit a nerve. Molly was a slim girl with glorious copper-coloured hair, falling in waves around attractive green eyes, in a delicate pale face. Yet, like so many girls, she hated what she saw in the mirror. How she longed to change what she saw as her 'ginger' hair, and to lose the freckles on her nose and cheeks.

Molly knew the nasty online posts had to be one or more of the girls at school, but who? They were all smiles to her face. Online was different. They were anonymous, and could say what they liked. No one could trace their cruelty back to them. They had free licence.

The dark-haired one is hot! Why is she friends with a carrot?

Rabbits will be pleased Molly won!

The comments were meaningless, but not to a self-critical girl, still grieving for her mother.

I wonder if Molly's mum was a carrot top too?

Molly shoved her phone away and howled silently into her pillow.

Chapter 12
Hazel Investigates

No one in the Greenwood family could understand why Molly's joy at winning the art prize had been so short-lived. By the next day, she appeared quiet and withdrawn, refusing to explain why. Anyone asking questions had their head bitten off. Billy and his father put it down to typical teenage behaviour and the anniversary of losing their mother. Molly was moody at the best of times, so it appeared she had just reverted to her normal behaviour.

Hazel had listened carefully to the conversations, waiting for clues. The guinea pig had also watched Molly on her phone. She had begun to think that the source of her unhappiness lay with that. All she needed was a chance to look more closely at the device.

Through close observation, Hazel had noted that Molly either used her thumb print to unlock her phone or typed in a four digit code. Molly was lazy enough to use the same number four times, so Hazel had soon worked it out.

Sometimes, Molly would sit Hazel on her knee whilst she used her phone, giving the piggy a chance to watch closely what she did. One particular icon on the screen seemed to hold the key. It was a blue and red question mark, and it was this that seemed to cause the distress whenever Molly pressed it.

At home, Molly was never separated from her phone, even in sleep. It seemed to live in her hand. It was her constant companion, but not one that seemed to give any pleasure.

The chance to look at her phone though seemed an impossibility – until that is a letter arrived through the post from *Morecaston High School.*

The headteacher had finally lost patience with the disruption cause by mobile phones in school. Numerous times, there had been incidents involving pictures being taken in the classroom and posted online. *All* phones were now to be left at home or be confiscated for one month.

Molly had been furious. She begged her father to object. To her horror, Mr Greenwood told her he would do no such thing. It would do her good to take a break from her device for at least a few hours each day.

Hazel's ears pricked up with interest as she overheard this heated exchange. Maybe a chance to look at Molly's mobile would present itself after all.

Sure enough, the precious phone was now at home in Molly's bedroom, on her desk. With everyone out at school or work, Hazel was able to hitch a ride on Skip's back, and visit Molly's room. Once in, she could access the top of the desk easily via a pile of boxes next to it, and was soon sitting looking at the phone.

She breathed deeply and concentrated upon the task in hand. She remembered that Molly always began by pressing a button at the bottom of the screen. Hazel did this as hard as she could with her toe. The screen lit up. Success! A keypad of numbers appeared.

Next, she remembered that Molly would press four times on the number 8.

She pressed the 8 on the screen four times with her toe. Nothing happened. She tried again, using two toes. Nothing. She breathed deeply through her rising frustration and tried once more, this time using the fleshy part of her paw. It worked. An array of small pictures appeared.

Hazel felt a thrill of excitement at her achievement. Never before had she even touched a piece of human technology, and now here she was, operating a smartphone.

Full of pride in herself, she glanced through the icons, searching for the blue and red question mark that Molly pressed so often. Finally, she found it.

She pressed the icon. The screen changed and *AskMe* opened up.

Hazel laughed gleefully at first, but her mirth was short-lived. She saw the words, *CarrotTopMollyGreenwood,* and began to read the posts which filled the screen:

Can carrots have freckles? Of course they can, 'cos Molly Greenwood does!

What's the difference between Molly Greenwood and a rotten carrot? Not a lot!

They went on and on. Hazel read them through with increasing horror. She had seen Molly scroll up and down with her fingertip, but she did not even attempt to do so. She had seen enough. Poor Molly. The secret of why she was so unhappy had now been revealed.

Chapter 13
A Girls' Afternoon

FRIDAY had finally arrived. After a long week at school, Molly was in her bedroom with Priscilla, who had accompanied her home after art club. Priscilla was now commiserating with Molly over the nasty online campaign. The two friends had spent the past ten minutes speculating over who the likely culprit might be.

From under the bed, Hazel the guinea pig was listening. With her usual determination, she had now learnt to climb the stairs on her own, and had slipped up to Molly's room whilst no one was looking. The small piggy was hoping to pick up some clues on who might be posting the nasty online comments.

Priscilla had brought her makeup kit and hairstyling tools to cheer her friend up with a makeover. As she unpacked her schoolbag, Molly noticed a small medal on a ribbon amongst the items.

"What did you win that for?" she asked.

"Oh, it's not mine," Priscilla explained, smiling sadly. "It's my mum's." She picked up the medal and held it in her hand, stroking it affectionately. "She was a gymnastics champion when she was younger. I keep it to remind me of her."

Molly smiled in sympathy. She knew her friend's mother had left home years ago and married again, leaving Priscilla to be brought up by her father.

"It helps to have a special something to remember them by, doesn't it?" said Molly quietly. She gestured to a wooden ornament on a nearby shelf. "That was a piece of driftwood my mum picked up on the beach, last time we were on holiday. My dad made it into a dragon for her." Her voice tailed off as she relived that day in her mind.

I wish my dad could be more like yours," said Priscilla sadly. She frequently complained to Molly about her father as he worked long hours, spending little time with her. It left her feeling rather alone and unloved.

"Anyway," said Priscilla brightly, "come on, enough sad memories. I came here to cheer you up. What shall we do first, hair or makeup?

"Hair!" said Molly vehemently "Shall I dye mine dark brown like yours?

"No," said Priscilla smiling, "be yourself!"

Hazel watched the two friends experimenting with different hairstyles, and shrieking with laughter. They tried plaits, pony tails, buns and hair grips, finally coming up with a new look for them both to share. The small guinea pig began to wish she had a sister of her own. It had all seemed such fun.

It was soon time for Priscilla to go home. Before she did so, the girls took a selfie of themselves smiling together, and posted it online.

The verdict came later that evening.

Has everyone seen carrot top's new look? It seems she's become Priscilla number two!

So, you think you can be as pretty as Priscilla, do you, Molly Greenwood?

Does anyone else have a vegetable for a twin?

Perhaps she should dye her hair to match Priscilla's too? Unless she wants to stay a carrot top forever!

Chapter 14
The Wasps

It was a warm, peaceful Monday, and the Greenwoods had each gone about their usual business for the day. Hazel and her family were out on the sunny lawn, with Skip and Madam Pom for company.

Madam Pom was having yet another snooze, and Skip was sniffing around the hedge, whilst Alfie and his younger brother were playing chase through the yellow tunnels, under the watchful eye of Mama. Hazel had gone for a wander on her own, down the far end of the garden.

She was finding solace where the marble statuettes stood.

It was hard to believe that the solid stone ornaments came to life at evening time, and transformed into the colourful figures of Godfrig, Merriel, Fion and Oro. It was even more special when the Full Moon came, and the Moon Queen transformed to join them too. Just being around the marble figures gave Hazel great comfort.

Her thoughts turned to Piggy Papa again. Previously, the Moon Queen had made her feel so much better, describing how Papa was still watching over her, often walking by her side. She knew now it was good to think happy thoughts of him as it made his memory clearer and brighter, like a flame given new strength.

Yet it was still sad that he was unable to live this new life with his family. How he would have loved to explore this garden, and enjoy the comfort of their warm, spacious hutch in the outhouse. The delicious secret of their hidden doorway to the garden would have appealed to him so much. It was from Papa that Hazel had inherited her adventurous spirit.

Her sadness at missing him joined with the worries over the continued nastiness to Molly, and weighed heavily upon her mind. Nevertheless, she slowly became aware of a loud buzzing sound. She looked around for the source of the harsh noise and saw that three wasps had settled on an apple blossom stem close by.

"Why, I do believe we have found the *Special One*," the first wasp announced.

Hazel looked at the insect with annoyance. She didn't care for the sneering tone in which it spoke, and was irritated at having her thoughts interrupted.

"Who are you?" she asked rather testily.

"Us? Oh, we're nobodies compared to *you*," came the reply from another of the wasps.

"Okay," replied Hazel drawing in a sigh, "Well whoever you are, I don't feel like talking, thank you very much. Goodbye."

She turned to leave, but the wasps began to follow her, circling around above her head.

"Don't go," the third one said with mock sadness. "We want to know so much more. I mean, how come you are supposed to be so *special* when you just don't look it?"

Hazel was taken aback at this. "How do you expect me to look?" she retorted hotly.

"Well, different at least," said the first wasp.

"Yeah, or just less *ordinary* would do," added the second.

The third insect flew down onto the grass near Hazel and looked pointedly at her front paws. "Your feet are certainly different," it said.

The other two joined it on the grass and stared at Hazel's feet.

"Yuck! They look positively weird – look at her long toes!"

Hazel flinched and pulled her front paws in beneath her. She had never liked the shape of her front feet.

She was in no mood to deal with this now. She turned

her back on the wasps and headed over in the direction of her family.

"Oh dear!" they called after her. "Is the *special* one crying *special* tears?"

With that, they flew back up into the air.

Ziggy, Zizzi and Zanna were three wasps who enjoyed tormenting others. It helped them bond with each other and was a fun way to pass the time.

They felt rather bitter at the way humans treated them. Their nest had been destroyed and they had found themselves out in the world without their companions. In every garden they visited, they were ushered away with the flap of a hand. People shouted and screamed when they appeared, and many children cried. Many of their relatives had been killed in jam traps. The world was hostile to them, and now they were finding comfort in each other's company. If the world was going to give them pain, they would repay it in full.

Hazel's emotional reaction had pleased them. They buzzed happily at their triumph and looked around for further fun. They spotted Alfie and Little Rufus, but they were in the company of Piggy Mama, Skip and Madam Pom. They preferred to pick on those alone, so the numbers were in their favour.

They left the garden and headed off to have fun elsewhere, but vowed to return. There was much more sport to be had here.

The next day, return they did. This time, they spotted Little Rufus on his own. A sparrow had landed on the lawn nearby, so the youngest guinea pig had chased over to look at it more closely. He had a great sense of curiosity and liked to investigate anything new. A juicy clump of grass had caught his eye. He needed to get to that and enjoy it before Alfie spotted it too.

Zizzi, Ziggy and Zanna saw their chance. They circled around the youngest piggy.

"Hello, little fellow," Ziggy called down.

Little Rufus stopped and looked up at them.

"You're rather dirty for a white guinea pig, aren't you?" said Zanna.

"Don't you ever wash your face?" asked Zizzi.

Little Rufus was shocked. "Of course I wash my face," he said huffily. "Mama showed me how to do that with my front paws."

The three venomous insects knew they had hooked another victim.

"Oh, your mama showed you, did she? She can't be a very good mother then, can she? How come you have a splodge of brown dirt over one eye?"

"It's a patch of colour, not dirt!" said Little Rufus angrily, his bottom lip trembling. He didn't like these wasps at all and hated them saying nasty things about Mama.

Not knowing how to cope with them, the young guinea pig scurried away to the safety of the yellow tunnels. In there, the wasps could see him frantically rubbing at his face with his front paws. They were about to pursue him further when they spotted Piggy Mama heading over to check on her son, and decided to leave it there.

Their fun here was done. They'd had a reaction and it had made their day. It made them feel important, and gave each one a sense of achievement. It was delicious fun to share between them and talk over later.

This continued for days. The trio of wasps visited the Bowood garden as often as they could. It was becoming their favourite place of fun. Once they had had enough of upsetting small children in other gardens, and annoying people walking along in the sunshine, they would head for the Bowood garden where their sport had become so sweet.

Today, Alfie had caught their eye. He was having a snooze beneath the shade of a bush, after chasing his brother through the tunnels.

The wasps made their way over to where he lay.

"Hey, *tufty*, wake up!" Ziggy called down as she buzzed over the head of Alfie.

The guinea pig jolted awake and looked up, slightly confused.

"What?"

"Why have you got a funny white tuft on your head? It looks like the colour's disappeared between your ears!"

Alfie looked up in annoyance at the flying insects. His voice was angry and upset. "Go away!" he shouted crossly. "I like my fur!"

"Why are you getting so angry when we mention it then? We were only having a joke," said Zizzi slyly. "Can't you take a joke? Don't you ever laugh?"

"Of course I can take a joke if it's funny," he retorted fiercely. "You're the jokes with your silly black and yellow bodies!"

The wasps buzzed in delight at his angry reaction. This was just the sort of game they enjoyed. They had quickly found a subject that got Alfie fired up.

They buzzed around him some more.

"So, we're ugly, are we?" said Zizzi. "At least we look like each other. You don't look like the other guinea pigs, do you? They don't have a weird tuft on their heads!"

"In fact," added Zanna, "I've never seen another guinea pig like you."

Ziggy joined in the fun, "We have visited *many* gardens, and seen lots of other guinea pigs. I definitely haven't seen a weird white tuft like that on any of them!"

This was a lie, but Alfie was not to know that.

"Get lost, ugly bugs!" was the best reply he could think of before running off to re-join his family.

As he ran up the garden, the painful words of the wasps played on his mind. Did everybody think that about him? Was his fur odd? Was he really the only one who had a white tuft between his ears? Alfie went to find the safety of the tunnel. He could not let anyone else see him upset.

The insects turned their attention elsewhere.

Madam Pom had appeared out of the dog flap and was sitting on the floor in front of the house, enjoying the sunshine.

Buoyed by their recent success, the wasps tried their usual tactics. Ziggy went first, "Hey, *fluffy head*!"

The insult did not even register with Madam Pom. She had not realised they were talking to her. Some silly buzzing insects were not something she even noticed.

The wasps moved in closer and landed on the ground near Madam. Zanna had a go this time, "Oi, you! *hairy face*!"

By now, The pedigree Pomeranian had realised their comments were directed at her. If there was one thing Madam Pom did not lack, it was confidence in herself. After all, she was Madam Pom Pom de Belvedere Dancing Queen, top of her breed at the Kennel Association of Great Britain. It would take more than three silly buzzing insects to make her doubt herself in any way.

Madam really could not be bothered to reply, especially in this warm sunshine. She looked disdainfully down at the insects, then shut her eyes and settled down for a sleep, her head on the ground between her front paws.

Not getting a response was a new experience for the trio of wasps. It was not one they liked. They moved closer to the fluffy dog, ready to try again.

Zizzi crawled over to her front paw.

She was about to offer another waspish barb when Madam opened one eye.

Without warning, the dog suddenly flicked her head to the side and snapped up Zizzi in her jaws. She kept her mouth firmly shut with the insect buzzing angrily inside.

Zanna and Ziggy did not know what to do. They could only look on in horror as they heard their companion's cries of distress.

They had no reason to fear. Within moments, Madam stood up, opened her mouth, and dropped the insect on the ground. She then calmy settled down once more, with her head between her paws, and continued her snooze in the sunshine, a knowing smile upon her face.

Zizzi picked herself up, feeling more than a little humiliated. She was furious at being treated in this way. The dog was too big to take on and too furry to sting. She needed to make herself feel better.

Never mind, the perfect opportunity had just presented itself. "Come on," she said to Ziggy and Zanna, "we have more work to do."

For further down the garden was their next victim...

Chapter 15
Hazel's Plan

Skip was happily sniffing around the bottom of the hedge bordering the Bowood garden as he so often loved to do. He was following the scent trail of a squirrel, and was engrossed in his search.

Zizzi, Ziggy and Zanna headed in his direction.

They buzzed around his head. "Hey, dog!"

Skip looked up in surprise and wagged his tail. He was always pleased to have company of any kind. He looked up expectantly. "Hello!" he said cheerily.

Zizzi was feeling particularly bitter after the encounter with Madam Pom and hence was at her most vindictive.

"How come you have a *brown* nose?" she asked spitefully.

Skip merely looked back puzzled. "Pardon?" he replied politely.

"You heard, deaf ears!" she said sharply. "I asked why you have a stupid *brown* nose?"

Skip looked troubled. "What's wrong with that?" he asked simply.

"Dogs' noses are meant to be black!" replied Zizzi. "Everyone knows that!"

Zanna joined in at this point to assist. She landed on the grass near Skip's foot.

"Guess what, everybody? His paw pads are brown too! Weird or what?"

The three wasps sniggered. The look of hurt in the small orange dog's eyes only spurred them on. It signalled success. It demonstrated their power over others, and stopped them feeling so worthless.

Skip was such a kind animal. He was well used to pointed comments from Madam Pom about not being a pedigree, but what he couldn't understand was anyone being cruel and unkind just for the sake of it - especially when they were strangers who didn't even know him.

Worse was to come.

"We hear you were a stray," said Zizzi, even more unkindly.

"Yeah, found roaming around like nobody wanted you," added Zanna.

"How did that feel?" asked Ziggy. "How did it feel to be *nobody's* pet?"

Skip's ears went flat. His curled tail straightened and drooped. His cheerfulness had gone. He felt quite out of sorts. The small orange dog had no idea how to respond. He merely dropped his head low and ran up the garden, intent on getting to the safety of the house as quickly as he could.

The trio of wasps watched him go with satisfaction, especially Zizzi, who now had some sense of self-worth back.

Smarting from the painful stinging comments which now filled his mind and stole his happiness, Skip pushed through the dog flap of the kitchen door. He padded across to his comfy bed and curled up next to his favourite chew toy. He shut his eyes to sleep and block out the pain.

Ziggy, Zizzi and Zanna headed off, pleased once more with their day's work.

But Hazel had been watching them.

And she had a plan.

She had been listening carefully to the kitchen radio that very morning, and heard something quite momentous which had made her sit up and listen.

The humans were talking about an exciting event - an event that, if used right, might just solve their problem perfectly. Hazel knew she would need to do some careful calculations.

There was no time to waste. Her brain whirred into action. By observing the Greenwoods' daily routines, she had a good sense of the days of the week. She could judge the time too from the natural signs taught by Grama Lizzy – the position of the sun in the sky, which flowers had their blooms open or closed, and the behaviour of the birds and the insects.

Friday would be the big day.

Friday dawned warm and breezy, with clear skies. The humans were excited and expectant.

So was Hazel.

The Greenwoods had left the house early. The special event was something they had decided to enjoy elsewhere, so the coast was clear.

Hazel had explained things carefully to the other animals in the family. They each understood the need to watch from a safe distance, keeping well out of sight.

The night before, Hazel had visited the sprites and enlisted Godfrig's help. At his request, Neavus the mole was now hard at work beneath the lawn of Bowood, in the exact spot required.

The guinea pig had put aside a small sweet juicy strawberry, provided by Billy for breakfast that morning. She now carried it down the garden to just the right place on the lawn.

She was desperately hoping that the wasps would keep to their usual visiting times – it was crucial to the plan.

Sure enough, after a short wait, a familiar buzz sounded in the air. The three wasps appeared.

Hazel began to nibble on the sweet, red, juicy strawberry.

"What have you got there, *Special One*?" Ziggy called down.

Hazel looked innocently up at them. "It's my breakfast," she replied.

Sensing some fun was to be had, the trio of insects immediately joined her on the lawn.

She looked up at them with a worried look on her face. "Please don't take my beautiful strawberry," she begged, gazing at the wasps with pleading eyes. "We don't get them very often."

"Oh, I think you could still share, *Special One*," replied Zizzi.

"Okay," Hazel announced in a sad, resigned tone. "You finish it off for me. I was getting full anyway."

Hazel was keeping a very close eye on the signs around her. Everything would depend on timing. She could not get this wrong. She just needed to wait a few moments more ...

She watched, hardly daring to breathe, as the wasps feasted greedily on the crimson fruit.

Then, she felt a change in the air.

The time was drawing closer.

Hazel now adopted a rather different tone. She spoke with a voice full of confidence, "You have had your fill, wasps. Now listen to my words."

Her change of voice made Ziggy, Zizzi and Zanna look up sharply from their feast.

"This is the last time you will visit this garden," said Hazel forcefully.

"Is that right?" scoffed Zanna loudly, as the other two giggled nastily.

"Beware," continued Hazel gravely, "as you yourselves have said, I am the *Special One*, and that gives me *special* powers – dark powers."

"Oh, yes?" sniggered Zizzi looking sideways at her fellow wasps.

"Never enter this garden again," commanded Hazel, "or I will use the full force of my powers on you. Promise now!"

"What? We don't have to listen to *you!*" sneered Zizzi.

At that moment, there was a rumbling in the soil beneath the spot where the wasps sat. As they looked down in alarm, the earth began to cave in beneath them and a hole appeared, swallowing up what remained of the sweet, juicy strawberry.

The three insects had to fly up in haste before they too disappeared after it.

Hazel breathed a sigh of relief. Thankfully, Neavus the mole had done his job down below with exact precision. She stared hard at Ziggy, Zizzi and Zanna.

"Let that be a warning to you, wasps. Do not mess with *The Special One*. As you have seen, I can take the earth from beneath your feet."

"Ha!" replied Ziggy, from above. "It will take more than that to scare us, stupid guinea pig. We have wings to escape such things!"

There was a noticeable tremble in her voice, however. The confidence of the trio was clearly shaken. Their bravado was not nearly as convincing as before. What more was this guinea pig able to do?

"Last warning," said Hazel calmly. "That was merely a taster."

She was measuring her words carefully. The time was almost right. Now she desperately needed Nature to play her part.

"Will you go and stay away," she asked, "or do I have to do my worst?"

"We'll take your worst!" shouted Zanna, from the safety of the air.

"Very well!" replied Hazel.

At that moment, the light in the garden took on a strange hue. The bright summer sunshine began to fade. Something most strange was happening.

The birds in the trees and bushes twittered and then fell silent.

The wasps too were now quiet and unsure.

The silence increased as the light faded further, slowly, slowly, slowly...

Gradually, the sun disappeared from sight, until a cold, terrifying darkness fell upon the garden.

It was as if the sun had been switched off like one of the humans' light bulbs.

Ziggy, Zanna and Zizzi were terrified.

"What have you done?!" Zizzi screamed.

"I have made the sun disappear," said Hazel imperiously, "and I can do worse to you. Never show your faces in this garden again if you value your lives!"

The wasps clung to each other, terrified and confused.

At last, the darkness began to lift, and a half light returned once more to the garden.

The wasps did not wait to hear more. They each took flight and buzzed away as fast as their wings could carry them.

Alfie, Little Rufus, Mama, Skip and Madam Pom all raced down the garden to join Hazel and celebrate her triumph.

The solar eclipse had done its job beautifully. For a few moments in time, the Moon had held power in the sky, perfectly positioned between the Earth and the Sun, halting the rays of light and warmth travelling from one to the other.

It was as if they had been forced to notice the Moon was there.

The world had witnessed a cosmic event, and in a small corner of the Earth, far, far, below, an equally important event had taken place - Hazel had brought peace and happiness back to the garden of Bowood.

Chapter 16
A Surprise Visitor

THE Full Moon brought The Moon Queen back once more.

As always, Her Majesty invited Hazel, Alfie, Mama, Little Rufus, Skip and Madam to join her in the garden. By the light of Fion's torches and the sweet music of Oro's reed pipe, the animals dined on the tasty delicacies supplied by Godfrig, washed down by the cool, refreshing water from Merriel's clamshell. They discussed all that had happened since the monarch's last visit.

The solar eclipse was the first topic of conversation. The Moon Queen was more than a little proud of her Lady in the Sky for showing her powers to the Earth and Sun. It was good to remind them that she was not to be ignored. The moonstone on the end of the monarch's staff glowed with pleasure.

The conversation then turned to the wasps. After congratulating Hazel on her clever solution to their bullying, The Moon Queen instructed Godfrig to summon the trio of wasps to her presence.

They arrived looking drowsy and apprehensive. The monarch looked down upon the three insects, her face as calm and serene as always, but her moonstone now showed an angry glow around the edges.

She opened her mouth to speak – but stopped abruptly.

For, at that moment, a bright yellow light lit up the garden. A feeling of heat filled the air and a bright golden figure appeared before the Moon Queen.

It was the figure of a maiden, much like herself, but unlike the gentle silver Moon Queen, this was a hot, fiery beauty. Beneath the sparkling crown on her brow, deep red locks of hair danced around her face like flames. Even her long golden gown seemed to blaze around her slender frame.

It was The Sun Queen.

"You know why I am here, Cousin Moon!" declared a sharp voice.

The Moon Queen was clearly startled, yet she gazed back at her fellow monarch with determination in her silvery-blue eyes. When she spoke, her tone was a little weary, as if she knew only too well why her relative had so suddenly appeared

"Indeed, Cousin Sun, I am only too well aware why you might be here."

"Then, you have clearly not learnt your lesson!" came the sharp reply. "Yet again Your Lady chose to eclipse mine today and deny the Earth her beautiful light!"

"May I remind you," responded The Moon Queen calmly, "I have no control over the solar eclipses, neither does My Lady. It is merely the position your lady and mine sometimes find themselves in. It is how they sit in the sky – for a few moments only, cousin."

"And look what happened in those few moments!" retorted the Sun Queen. "You saw how the flowers shut their blooms, how the beasts and birds stood still, how cold the Earth became!"

The aura of heat around the maiden became yet more fierce, as her own temperature seemed to rise with her anger. "Do I need to remind you that My Lady commands the skies and rules the day, every day, without fail? Your lady belongs in the dark. She comes and goes in the sky – sometimes she disappears completely to those below!"

The Sun Queen's anger seemed to increase as she spoke.

"And there is *no* such thing as *moon*light – your lady merely reflects the light of *My* Lady – yours produces nothing of her own!"

The Moon Queen made no attempt to interrupt as the fiery monarch's rage burned relentlessly.

"Without My Lady," declared The Sun Queen, "life on

Earth would cease. The plants and trees and grasses would no longer grow; the animals would die of hunger and Man too! She warms the Earth, she nourishes it, she affords it happiness. Your lady is merely a pale imitation. She may have eclipsed My Golden Lady for a short time today, but she will never take her place!"

The Sun Queen's eyes blazed. She stared in furious silence at The Moon Queen.

The Moon Queen sat with her eyes downcast, no longer looking at her fiery cousin, as if all fight had left her body, leaving her with no response to give.

The Sun Queen's eyes blazed once more, but receiving no response, she fumed, "I have said enough. I have no more reason to stay, so I will take my leave, but mark my words for future, cousin!"

With that, she vanished from sight as suddenly as she'd appeared. A haze of heat lingered on the spot where she had stood.

The Moon Queen's silver-blue eyes seemed full of silent pain.

Hazel and her companions had been rooted to the spot with fear as the royal drama had played out before them. The three wasps had fared no better.

Even the sprites had looked on in horror, unable to intervene in a power battle far beyond their control.

But now, as if the spell had been broken, Godfrig moved straight to the side of The Moon Queen, closely followed by Merriel, Fion and Oro. They offered her water, they fanned her face, they spoke gently, but all to no avail. For, to everyone's alarm, silver tears began to fall gently down her cheeks.

The Sun Queen's words had clearly wounded The Moon

Queen deeply. Hazel sensed her pain and felt her own eyes misting over in helpless sympathy for the queen who had done so much for her.

Hazel suddenly realised that Godfrig had disappeared. Her eyes scanned the garden to see where he could be. He was always the one to rely on, the one to organise and take control of any situation, but where was he now? Surely, he had not deserted Her Majesty in her hour of need?

Her fears were unfounded, for Godfrig now reappeared, striding across the lawn - with company. He walked beside none other than The Sage, The Chief of the Earth Sprites, Ruler of the Woods.

The ancient gnome had left his dominion of the ancient forest to stand before The Moon Queen. Hazel breathed a sigh of relief, for who else but someone of equal stature to The Moon Queen could bring a solution?

As he spoke, The Sage's very presence and his deep, warm voice of quiet authority, brought an immediate sense of calm.

"Problems, Majesty? "

The Moon Queen looked up as she heard his words. Her silver eyes seemed to brighten as she replied, "Indeed, Sage." She smiled gently back at him, with her usual serene smile, though the moonstone on her staff appeared to have lost its sparkle – a detail not lost on The Sage.

"Godfrig has told me enough, Majesty, so there is no need to revisit the pain of tonight's events. Perhaps we should concentrate first on calming everyone's feelings. I have something to assist.

With that, he produced a flagon of acorn wine. Godfrig produced some cups of acorn shell which The Sage filled with a pleasant yellow liquid, as Godfrig handed them out to all, including the wasps.

At The Sage's instruction, all those present in the garden sipped from the cups and listened to what he had to say next.

"Now," said The Sage, "let me draw your attention to these flowers at my feet." Everyone looked. Where The Sage stood, a clump of dandelions grew. In the cool, dark night air, their heads were tightly closed, allowing only a glimpse of the yellow petals hidden inside.

The Sage bent down and placed his weathered nutbrown hands around one of the closed heads. At his warm touch, the outer leaves relaxed and opened to reveal the pretty yellow bloom beneath. The other heads around opened up too.

"Did any of you notice this flower before I arrived?" asked The Sage

No one answered, for no one was sure. Were the dandelions there before? It would seem that no one could remember. The Sage smiled. "I thought not. We rarely pay them much attention, do we? "

He turned his brown eyes upon The Moon Queen and said, "These much-overlooked flowers, Majesty, can teach us all an important lesson. They have much to offer, as I'm sure you know, but we just tend to forget. "

The Sage paused, looking into the

eyes of The Moon Queen, "Before we remind ourselves, let me tell you one of my favourite stories, often told by the creatures of the wood. It recalls how these pretty blooms came by their marvellous qualities."

Godfrig brought The Sage a rock to sit upon, and then joined the others to listen in anticipation to what he had to say.

Chapter 17
The Oleander Tree

"ACCORDING to legend," began The Sage, "an attractive oleander tree was growing on the banks of a stream. A traveller passed by and spied its exquisite blooms of pure white. He wanted them for his sweetheart, but was far too idle to reach up high for each one. Instead, he produced an axe from his bag and felled the whole tree.

His thick gloves protected him from the poisons in the leaves, so he was able to take his fill of the fine, delicate flowers. He then went on his way, caring nothing for the destruction he had left behind.

The tiny fairies who lived upon the tree and tended to its every need, were left distraught. They could do nothing to save the tree and had to watch it die.

Now they had no purpose in life, with no tree to tend and watch over. Their sadness was overwhelming, so much so that they each lost the use of their wings. No longer could they even flutter through the air, or ride the currents of a gentle breeze.

The fairies knew they must find a new home, yet could not begin their search without the use of their wings. This could never return whilst their sadness weighed so heavily upon them. Their predicament was severe.

One fairy wandered afar through the grass and the flowers, full of melancholy. She paused to sit awhile upon the leaf of a dandelion, and take comfort from the joyful yellow beauty of the petals upon its head. The flower was patient and friendly, so she told her sad tale.

As she did so, a tiny tear rolled down her cheek and fell upon the leaf. The dandelion felt such pity for the fairy that it told her to rest beneath its leaves for the night, and by daybreak it would have an answer to her problem.

Early next morning, a drop of dew awoke the slumbering fairy. She turned to look for the beautiful yellow head of the flower, but it was gone. In its place was a feathery ball of the purest white.

As she gazed, one of the delicate feathery white heads broke free from the ball and floated in the air before her. At its top were hundreds of fine threads, which spread out upon the breeze, and at its lower end was a seed. The fairy instinctively understood. She stepped onto the seed and held on to its slender stem. Immediately, the feathery white threads caught the air and lifted the fairy up, up and up.

The fairy let out cries of joy which alerted her companions. They now gazed in wonder at her sailing through the air above their heads. They were bewildered at first, until further seed heads broke free and floated over in their direction. Each fairy caught hold of a delicate stem and climbed upon the seed at its foot. Soon all the fairies were airborne once more, feeling their old happiness return.

The fairy troupe was carried along to a young sapling of another oleander tree. It would be theirs to nurture and tend. In time, it grew big, and the fairies' happiness returned, along with the use of their wings.

Word spread amongst the fairy kingdom and reached its King and Queen. In return for its good deed, the dandelion, and all its kind, were granted special powers.

No matter how Man pulled them from the soil or cut them down, life would still be theirs. From the tiniest piece of root left behind, they would grow once more and return to life, standing yellow and proud."

The Sage had been watching the eyes of his audience closely as he told the tale of the fairies and the dandelions.

From their calm, relaxed expressions, he now sensed the time was right to pursue his real purpose. He did not turn his attention directly to The Moon Queen, but let his words seem as if they were for all who listened – in some sense they were.

"We all have much to learn from this simple bloom. The dandelion is not the most glamorous of flowers, despite its pretty yellow. Others take more of the glory – the roses with their perfect petals and exquisite perfume; the sun flowers with their tall spires and magnificent broad faces; even the apple blossoms with their dainty bells atop of graceful stems. Yet the dandelions are no less important."

The Sage smiled kindly at the Moon Queen as he continued, "Once the snowdrops have first shown the way, the dandelions are the next to emerge, their green buds forming before February is done.

Their golden petals soon follow, giving cheer to the world and reminding it of the warm summer days to come. Their nectar is not the richest nor the sweetest, but it helps sustain the first bumble bees taking flight, the hoverflies and the butterflies too. The dandelions feed the moth caterpillars and pollen beetles besides, well before the other flowers appear."

The Sage watched The Moon Queen carefully as he continued gently, "And when the dandelion blooms depart – they leave behind their snowy white seed heads to feed the grouse, the partridges and the pheasants. The seeds themselves give nourishment to our songbirds - the blackbirds and the goldfinches, the sparrows and the siskins."

The Sage's wise old eyes seemed to smile. He allowed his words to linger in the air for a few moments. As he did so, he reached down and took a petal from a dandelion bloom at his feet. He held it between his forefinger and thumb and announced, "Sometimes, we need reminding of our best qualities."

"Majesty, I think you have forgotten that Your Lady, The Moon, does many wonderful things."

He held out the delicate petal. "Godfrig, present this to Her Majesty." The earth sprite did as he was bid, and took the petal over to the Moon Queen, bowing his head in respect. The monarch took the petal in her slender, pale fingers.

"Let this first petal remind you, Majesty," said The Sage, "that the Moon controls the tides of the oceans here on Earth. Thanks to her, they are regular, predictable and dependable."

The Sage drew another petal and handed it to Merriel this time. As the water sprite presented it to The Moon Queen, The Sage continued, "Let this second petal remind you that it is Your Lady's gentle pull on the Earth which keeps it stable in the sky and turning smoothly. She gives Man his day, his month, his seasons. Without her, these would change beyond all recognition."

A further petal was placed in Fion's hand. She took her turn in carrying it to The Moon Queen whilst The Sage added, "Furthermore, without the Moon to reflect the light from the Sun, the night sky would be dark, black and cheerless, save for the tiny light from the stars."

Oro was handed the final petal. As he presented it to the monarch, The Sage announced, "And finally, the Moon is a constant friend to Man. He can look her in the face and take comfort from her presence in the darkest hour. He cannot do this with the Sun. Her glare is strong and unfriendly to the eye. Unlike the moderate Moon, the Sun is unpredictable with her many changing moods. She can be calm, cool and subdued one day, yet the next, she can blaze down upon the planet, burning and scorching all before her."

The Sage now stopped and waited patiently for The Moon Queen to take in his words of wisdom. She gazed down at the four dainty petals in her pale hand and smiled. The light had returned to her silver-blue eyes, and the moonstone atop her staff had regained its delicate sparkle.

"Thank you, Sage," she said.

Her words were quiet, simple and plain, but her soft silvery voice carried a depth of emotion which The Sage heard and understood.

Hazel had watched all this alongside the wasps. She felt like a shadow on the wall, with no significance of her own, a mere spectator at a performance of a show in which she played no part.

However, she was wrong, for The Sage now looked over in her direction. She swallowed hard in disbelief.

"My young friend, Hazel," he said, "we meet again."

Hazel could do no more than blink. Words seemed to fail her as her throat tightened.

The Sage understood and looked for no response. He carried on to say, "You too, I think, can take some lesson from the dandelion. For it is small and determined – much like you."

Hazel felt the colour run to her cheeks.

The Sage continued, "I wonder if the comments of others, in recent times, have made you doubt your own true worth."

At this, the three wasps shifted uncomfortably on the ground.

"Hazel," said The Sage, "I heard about your recent rescue of the young blackbird, who you kept from the jaws of a fearsome cat. That was quick thinking on your part. I fear you have forgotten the bravery you showed when you came with Godfrig to the Ancient Wood, and met with me in my home. That was a mighty journey for a small one like yourself."

The Sage looked towards Ziggy, Zizzi and Zanna. "Perhaps those who choose to demean you would like to try such an undertaking themselves."

The wasps flattened themselves to the ground.

"Or perhaps," The Sage said, "they too are failing to recognise their own good qualities. Feeling insecure does make us attack others, does it not, my tiny friends?"

The wasps exchanged puzzled glances.

"A happy individual does not cause pain to others," The Sage added.

"I know that Man does not admire you wasps as he does the exotic butterfly or the busy bumble bee, yet you are of equal worth. You eat the greenfly, the beetle larvae and the caterpillars, which would destroy his crops if you did not limit their numbers. You pollinate the flowers too, which colour his world, but does he thank you? No, he sees you as a pest to be destroyed – just like the dandelion."

The three wasps buzzed happily at his words.

"However," continued The Sage, "that is no excuse for venomous behaviour, wherein you sting, you wound, and you hurt."

The three wasps bowed their heads as The Sage's gentle, but firm voice continued, "Perhaps, if we were kinder to ourselves, and recognised our own true value, we might feel less inclined to be cruel to others around us."

The Sage now looked calmly at The Moon Queen. "Keep

those petals safe, Majesty, and never forget the lesson they teach us."

As he uttered his last words, he looked upwards. The Moon Queen, sprites, guinea pigs, Pomeranians and wasps all did the same. As they gazed, feathery white seed heads began to float and swirl through the air like a gentle fall of snow in summer.

When all present looked down again, The Sage was gone.

Chapter 18
The Committee Meeting

I⊤ was evening time in Brierley Bramble. John Greenwood was sitting in the back room of the local inn, *The Withered Oak*, awaiting the start of the Village Events Committee meeting. He had deliberately arrived early to have some peace and quiet from the high emotions at home.

The Withered Oak was his place of refuge. Its snug, cosy interior owed much to the solid oak beams in its low ceiling, provided by his ancestors before him.

On a Friday evening, after a long week of work, the master craftsman often enjoyed a fine tankard of ale there with friends, sitting by the warm flames in the generous fireplace. There was nothing like good conversation, and the comfort of rich hops and barley, for taking the edge off his troubles.

As he waited for the other members of the committee to arrive, his thoughts turned to the recent addition, Mrs Pepper. John was still bristling from the recent grilling he and Billy had received at Brierley Bramble Junior School. They had both been invited to attend a special governors' meeting, to explain the reasons for Billy's poor progress against his targets. Other struggling pupils and their parents had endured the same ordeal.

Mrs Pepper may only have filled the vacant chair of governors' position because no one else wanted it, but she was making it her own in a very short space of time.

It was her formidable organisational skills that had opened doors so quickly. She was available to do whatever needed doing, and always completed tasks exceptionally well. For this reason, she was now on the Events Committee too.

Mrs Pepper made it clear, early on, that she did not approve of the meeting taking place in an ale house, but recognised this was one battle she would not win. How ironic, John mused. The name of the inn had been in tribute to King Charles II, who had once hidden from enemy forces within the hollow of an ancient oak tree. When he claimed back the throne of England, the new monarch had reinstated the right to fun and merriment, after the killjoy Oliver Cromwell had imposed Puritan values across England. Somehow, John saw a connection there with Mrs Pepper.

In truth however, the villagers of Brierley Bramble had never stopped enjoying themselves. The return of the King simply meant it need no longer be hidden behind closed doors.

Many of the surrounding villages had named their taverns *The Royal Oak,* in tribute to the playful monarch who had used the much-loved English tree for refuge. The villagers of Brierley Bramble, however, never liked to do what the other villages did, so their tribute became *The Withered Oak* instead.

Besides, royalty was not generally something they had

much time for. They were respectful of it, but did not bow down to it unless they had to.

This was much like their attitude to the chapel. They worshipped not in the confines of its stone walls, but in the fields, the woodlands, the streams and hedges, in the skies overhead, and in the heavens stretching out endlessly above them.

The forthcoming carnival day was important for this reason, as it centred around the annual well dressing celebration. The ancient well on the edge of the village was decorated each year with mosaic style pictures, created from Nature's own materials. They gave thanks for the pure, clean water which had sustained the people of the village during the plague years.

It truly was the highlight of the year, enjoyed even more than May Day (by some a little too much, especially if they had work the next day).

For the locals, it was not merely gratitude for the precious drinking water; it was also a celebration of their freedom.

Many of the older generation loved to recount how their ancestors had been refused the right to graze their animals on the common land, and to forage for food in the local woods. Many centuries before, King William had gifted it all to some member of the landed gentry. Access had been denied from that day on, with the threat of gaol if they so much as set foot on the forbidden land.

Centuries later, the local squire had reinstated all rights, allowing all to roam at will, across the fields and woods. Freedom had come back to Brierley Bramble, and that was what the villagers loved to celebrate the most.

The festivities were the subject of today's meeting. Much hard work had happened over many weeks, and now, under the guiding hand of Mrs Pepper, it would all be marshalled into shape far quicker than ever before.

As John Greenwood waited, Betty arrived, soon taking up a seat beside him. She was closely followed by Agnes Frankie, Ernie Bostock, Cecilia Adebayo, Neville Frost and Sandeep Singh. All steeled themselves for the arrival of Hortense Pepper.

At precisely the right time, the lady herself swept in. She offered a curt greeting to those present and took her place at the table. Once her half-moon spectacles were on, and her pen was poised in her hand, it was down to business.

The meetings were now a lot less fun, with no time for idle chatter. They were clinical, to the point, and over in an hour, with everything on the agenda done and dusted.

With everything on the list ticked off, Mrs Pepper removed her spectacles, and clicked her elegant silver pen, before popping both into her large, black handbag. She rose from the table, bid the others good evening, and swept out the same way she had come in.

Everyone breathed a sigh of relief, the atmosphere relaxing immediately.

"Okay," said John Greenwood cheerily, rubbing his hands together, "I'll get the drinks in, shall I?"

Chapter 19
The Preparations Begin

Excitement was building in the village. The preparations for Carnival Day were a big part of the fun. The well dressing tradition stretched back generations and brought the whole village together.

The process followed the same steps each year. First, the heavy old wooden frames, made in times gone by John Greenwood's father, had been brought out of storage and were now soaking in the village stream.

Soon they would be removed, ready for the layer of soft, wet clay to be applied. The clay had to be ready at just the right time. It had to be neither too firm nor too soft. "You have to get the puddlin' right," the older folk always warned in stern voices.

And so, a select number of villagers, skilled at this particular task, would work just the right amount of water and salt into the clay, in the old tin baths kept specially for the purpose, in Farmer Jack Lewis's barn.

Children were invited to assist, by trampling the clay beneath their feet, which they happily did, squealing with delight at the goo squishing between their toes.

With great reverence, the clay was then applied around

the pegs in the frames, and carefully smoothed over, before those with the right artistic skills would etch the agreed designs into the clay surface.

The adults and children alike loved the colouring-in part which followed. They would pick flowers, plants, herbs, twigs, pine cones, berries and anything else growing, which could be harvested for the purpose of filling in the pictures in the clay. It was then that the designs came to life, with crimson and creamy yellow petals pressed into the clay, next to fresh greens, bright oranges, deep blues and purples. The theme beloved of the villagers was always wildlife and nature.

Everything was now ready. Each generation had played its part. One thing they all knew how to do in Brierley Bramble was enjoy themselves, and it would take more than Oliver Cromwell or even the mighty Mrs Pepper herself to ever put a stop to that.

Chapter 20
The Dog Show

I⟨T⟩ was a dazzling summer's day, and the world was smiling in the sunshine. The bright light reflected off each and every surface as if in celebration. A haze of happiness hung over the earth, as people slowed down and relaxed, taking time to stop and notice the beauty around them. Everyone seemed to like each other more on a day like today.

The day of the carnival had finally arrived. Earlier that morning, back at Bowood, Hazel had overheard a conversation between Billy and Molly about a pet show being part of the festivities. She recognised a perfect opportunity for dealing with an ongoing situation in the house.

For Madam Pom had been even snappier and more ill-tempered than usual. She had buried Skip's beloved chew toy in the garden at least three times that week, chewed up the doormat, and been extra caustic with the guinea pigs. It was all in protest at being thwarted in her attempts to gain access to the Bowood garden strawberry patch again.

Quite why she wanted to do so, nobody knew, for she was heavily allergic to strawberries. If she ate even part of one, her face would swell up, her eyes would become red and inflamed, and her airways part-restricted, causing her snorty breathing to be louder than ever. It required an injection from Constance Clark, the vet, to calm her alarming symptoms down and bring her back to normal.

However, despite the dreadful consequences, Madam Pom could not control her addiction. She remained intoxicated by the mere aroma of the sweet, red globes of fruit. As the pedigree Pomeranian rarely learnt from her experiences in life, she would simply return to the strawberry patch, time  and time again, to break her way in by any means possible.

Mr Greenwood had finally put an end to her escapades by double-fencing the strawberry patch in strong oak timbers, so blocking her access once and for all. Madam Pom was now safe from further frightful allergic reactions, but much grouchier as a result.

Fortunately, Hazel had seen an opportunity to distract Madam Pom and stop her from being such an ill-tempered nuisance. She found a flyer which had come through the letterbox that morning. It was from a dog grooming parlour in Morecaston. *Pam's Pooch Parlour* promised to transform any dog's looks into those of a champion. To emphasise this point, a proud Poodle with neatly trimmed fur, and a superimposed crown, was pictured alongside a huge trophy of gleaming gold.

Hazel snapped it up with her teeth. She primed her brother Alfie on the plan, before the two guinea pigs set off to the kitchen, where the Pomeranian lay snoozing on her plump, cushioned bed. She was tired out from digging holes and making yet more futile break-in attempts on the straw-berry patch.

Hazel and Alfie positioned themselves nearby. Hazel ensured she would have the dog's attention by knocking a fallen teaspoon against her empty food bowl, left over from breakfast time.

Madam opened a hopeful eye. Upon being disappointed, she growled in protest at this dreadful interruption to her beauty sleep. Hazel seized her chance.

"Alfie," she announced, so Madam could hear, "have you seen this advert for today's dog show?"

Alfie had to stifle a giggle as he replied, "Dog show?"

Madam Pom sat up immediately, "What's that you said?"

"Oh, Madam Pom, haven't you heard?" said Hazel in mock surprise. Fully aware that Madam could not read a word, Hazel slipped the flyer for the grooming parlour beneath the pedigree's nose. "Here's the advert. Not just any dog show – it's *the* dog show - Kroft's!"

The effect was instant.

"Kroft's?" exclaimed Madam, jumping to her feet. She stared at the picture of the proud dog on the leaflet. "You mean, the world famous international dog show?!"

Yes," said Hazel. "It's not in London this year; it's coming to our village, and Our Boy Billy is going to enter you!"

The lack of logic or sense in this was lost on Madam, who only had a hazy understanding of the human world at the best of times. She was instantly beside herself with indignation. "Why was I not informed of this before?!" she demanded to know.

Madam's mind raced. This was her big chance. *She* knew she was the top of her breed with the Kennel Association of Great Britain, but no one else seemed to recognise this fact.

If she - Madam Pom Pom de Belvedere Dancing Queen - was officially crowned today (as was only right) then inferior dogs like Skip would be forced to give her the respect she truly deserved. She announced that she was off to make 'the necessary preparations'.

Hazel and Alfie had no idea what they might be, and really didn't care, as long as it stopped her from making life a misery for them all. Hazel knew that Billy was intending to enter each of them in the pet show that day, as there was a small cash prize on offer. He needed to replenish the contents of his piggy bank, before his dad found out, after spending it all on sweets. So, the handsome Madam Pom did stand a chance of getting some sort of award – just not from Kroft's.

Chapter 21
Carnival Day

Pᴿᴼᴄᴱᴱᴰᴵᴺᴳˢ were well under way at the Brierley Bramble well dressing carnival. The ancient well, on the edge of the village, was resplendent with a huge wooden frame, filled to the brim with colourful petals, depicting the scene of a crop gatherer, above the slogan: 'We thank Nature for our bounty'. Smaller unofficial boards of similar natural scenes sat alongside it.

Behind this, the green space of the old estate was filled with various tented stalls, circling a central arena. An assortment of goods were on offer, from homemade foods, farm produce, ales and ciders, to corn dollies, woven baskets and other items crafted by locals.

Smaller rings nearby housed the children's play area, junior well dressing displays and other events.

The air was alive with the excited chatter of children, alongside the cheerful conversations of villagers exchanging views and catching up on the latest gossip. Everyone, from young and old, was wearing their best summer clothes with cheerful expressions to match.

John Greenwood had been tasked with the job of judging the children's well dressing competition, and so was busy behind the main arena, leaving Billy to enter the pet show under Molly's watchful eye.

Molly had charge of Madam and Skip, whilst Billy had the guinea pigs in their carry cage. Brother and sister sat side by side on seats at the edge of the arena, waiting patiently for the pet competitions to begin. The happy atmosphere of the occasion meant neither felt inclined to bicker with the other, at least for the time being. Molly had even put away her phone and was managing to smile.

On the other side of the arena, Betty was busy on her homemade foods stall, assisted by Jim and Agnes Frankie. As in previous years, she had provided a splendid array of her finest creations, many crafted from the natural items she had foraged in the local woods and fields.

The villagers looked forward with anticipation to whatever new recipes she had come up with each year. There was always something fresh and different. Yet again, Betty had not disappointed. Alongside her traditional (and much-loved) hedgerow jelly, dandelion jam, elderflower cordial and cucumber lemonade, there were preserves of apricots with parsley, apple with pear and coriander, plus raspberry jam with basil and thyme, to name just a few. The busy queue at the stall told its own tale. It was almost as popular as the ale tent.

Mrs Pepper stood and watched. She had already inspected the weird and wonderful array of jams, chutneys, cordials and lemonades with increasing disapproval. Why did people have to interfere with the traditional ways? You knew where you were with jams of pure blackberry, apricot or strawberry. Surely, they were sufficient?

She held a deep distrust of people like Betty, people who interfered with the natural order of things, who didn't do things *right*. They went against what was expected, and that made her fearful and nervous. Their ways could lead to chaos and insecurity.

Such fears always brought out the worst in her character. When no one was looking, she had helped herself to a large jar of Betty's strawberry and oregano blossom jelly, to investigate later – certainly not to eat. For now, she hid it beneath the back skirt of the tent around Betty's stall.

Straightening her sun hat and smoothing her dress, Mrs Pepper got herself ready for her main task of the day. She had put herself forward as the official judge for the dog section of the pet show. She had such a forceful character that no one on the organising committee had had the energy to argue with her and compete for the position. If she was so keen, she could have it, was the commonly held view. Besides, if she was busy doing that, she would be out of everybody else's way, for at least part of the time.

Mrs Pepper did not actually like dogs, and knew very

little about them, but she *did* like feeling important. She particularly relished the feel of a clipboard in her hands, with her special, expensive, silver pen poised over a score sheet, knowing her judgement would make or ruin someone's day.

Impatiently, she waited as the competition for best fruit and vegetables took place, judged by Mrs Kinder. When it finally ended, she watched the various breeds of dogs being led over to the display tables.

Mrs Pepper had insisted that the owners left their pets unaccompanied, on the special low display tables set up for the purpose, with identification numbers attached to their collars or harnesses. That way, she could hide the fact that she didn't know what she was doing.

Many locals were only too happy to keep their distance from her. A number of them were parents, still smarting from their 'interviews' with The Brierley Bramble Junior School board of governors.

Clutching her clipboard, Mrs Pepper's hands trembled in anticipation at the power she would wield. From under the brim of her smart hat, she glanced at the expectant faces lining up with high hopes for their precious pets. She began to stroll around the tables, clicking the top of her smart silver pen.

Mrs Pepper took care to avoid any friendly licks from the assorted cockerpoos, spaniels, terriers, chihuahuas and other dogs, who sat beneath their sunshades, ready for her judgements to be made. They all looked the same to her uninterested eye. She paused at each table, just for effect, feigning interest in each animal, pretending to note its features as if scoring each one by some secret criteria.

Eventually, she came to Madam Pom, her orange coat looking splendid in the sun light, alongside the fine ruff around her neck and her magnificent fluffy tail. Mrs Pepper paused to look her in the eyes. The proud Pomeranian gave the woman a haughty look. Mrs Pepper returned an icy stare. Each sensed the contempt felt by the other and neither liked it in the least.

By the time Mrs Pepper turned away, one fact was certain, Madam Pom would be winning no prizes from her.

Her eyes fell instead on Skip, who sat obediently on the next table along. A slight smile warmed Mrs Pepper's glacial expression. Now there was a dog she liked the appearance of. The innocent, good natured look on his face presented no challenge to her authority. He had a brown nose too which, for some reason, took her fancy.

It was hot and Mrs Pepper wanted to be out of the sun, so her mind was made up. She noted down his number, with her special silver pen, and clicked it with satisfaction, before slotting it neatly into the top of the clipboard. Job done.

She handed in the score sheet, and then took herself off to the back of the homemade goods stall, where she had hidden the large, offensive jar of strawberry and oregano blossom preserve. She glanced around to ensure no one was looking before retrieving it from its hiding place. Like a scientist investigating a deadly specimen in a laboratory, she held it at arm's length whilst gingerly unscrewing the lid.

To many others, the aroma released at that moment would have been fruity, delicate and interesting, but to Hortense Pepper it was vile. She dropped it in disgust. The robust jar survived the fall, but its contents spilt out in a large mound on the grass. Mrs Pepper picked up a nearby plastic chair and placed it over the sticky mess, before slipping away as if nothing had happened.

Soon the results were announced over the loud speaker. The rosettes were brought out, and the large red *Best in Show* rosette was bestowed upon Skip with great reverence by Mrs Pepper herself, with a fixed smile of cerise lipstick.

Hazel, Alfie, Mama and Little Rufus were still in their carry cage, which sat at Billy's feet. The guinea pigs could only watch in horror as the large red rosette got clipped to Skip's harness.

Of course, they were pleased for him, but they would never hear the end of this. Life at Bowood would be hell for weeks. Hazel glanced fearfully at Madam Pom's table. She needn't have worried, for at that moment, the pedigree

Pomeranian was lying fast asleep, snoring thunderously. The heat of the sun had overcome her desperate bid to stay awake, ready to receive the top prize.

But what would they do when she awoke and learned of the result?

Chapter 22
Perfect Rupert

THE problem of what to do about Madam Pom was not Hazel's only concern that day.

She, and the other piggies, had been placed on one large table for the small animal competition, close to other cages also containing guinea pigs.

Hazel took a deep breath as she looked into the cage immediately next to theirs. For inside, was the most stunning guinea pig she had ever set eyes upon.

His long chestnut-brown fur had highlights of pure white. A shock of fur hung over one eye, adding to his perfect beauty. Hazel heard him addressed as Rupert – what a lovely name, she thought.

Hazel was entranced. Her heart thumped in her chest and her throat tightened with nervous tension at the thought of him even looking in her direction, never mind speaking to her.

This was not lost on Alfie or Little Rufus, who had both noticed her reaction to the piggy next door, and took great delight in sniggering at their sister's discomfort. Piggy Mama had to intervene for their sakes and move them to the other side of the cage. She knew how hot Hazel's temper could get when her brothers teased her too much.

The judging had finished without her even noticing. Her attention had been too caught up by her close proximity to Rupert.

Next thing she knew, a red rosette had arrived and was being attached to his cage. His owner, a small girl, could be heard saying, "Good boy, Rupert, I knew you could do it!"

"Wow, congratulations!" said Hazel warmly, through the bars of their cages, as she finally plucked up the courage to speak to him.

The long-haired guinea pig turned a proud eye towards her and said loftily, "It was only to be expected. I am after all the best looking guinea pig here."

Hazel smiled and gave a nervous giggle, thinking he was joking, but soon realised he was actually quite serious.

To her surprise, Rupert began to scoff at the other guinea pigs nearby. "I mean what chance did *she* have over there?" he asked, indicating a smooth Californian guinea pig, a couple of cages away. "She's got funny shaped ears and looks like she's got bumblefoot in all four paws!"

The poor Californian overheard the loud comment and looked quite downcast.

Hazel was shocked by his unnecessary cruelty, and by the unfairness of his comments. The Californian guinea pig was sleek and glossy. She had a pretty face, with a friendly expression, and looked like the sort of piggy Hazel would happily talk to, given the chance. She could see very little wrong with her feet or her ears.

Rupert now turned his attention to a ginger rough-haired guinea pig who had the misfortune to be sharing a cage with him. "As for *spikey* here, who'd award *him* anything? His fur sticks up all over – he looks like he's been pulled through a hedge!"

Hazel instinctively drew her feet under her body before Rupert caught sight of them and started on her next.

Eventually, Rupert tired of speaking to Hazel and took himself off to the other side of his cage. The ginger piggy, labelled *spikey,* took his place and rolled his eyes to Hazel. "Thank goodness he's shut up at last."

Hazel smiled, feeling instantly at ease with this very different guinea pig. "Is he always like that?" she enquired.

"Oh yes," came the weary reply. "He looks perfect, doesn't he? Well, I can assure you, perfection is hard to live with."

Hazel looked around at the other piggies with their so called *bumble feet* and scruffy fur, and felt so much happier and relaxed. She sighed in relief and allowed her feet to show. The ginger piggy glanced down. Hazel's heart stopped.

"What lovely long toes you have," he said. "I bet they're really useful. I've got short, stubby ones!" he added with a wry smile, stretching his front paws out for her to see. "They look like chunks of carrot!"

Hazel instantly took to this piggy. He was warm and friendly with a nice sense of humour. Why on earth had she ever looked in the direction of Rupert the big-head?

She looked at the large rosette attached to the cage. That simple piece of ribbon and cardboard was so important to Rupert, but really meant very little to anyone else. He might be handsome to look at, but that was all there was to him. She actually felt rather sorry for the arrogant guinea pig. He was like another Madam Pom – and one of those was quite enough.

Hazel was about to ask the ginger piggy what his proper name was when a sudden commotion caught everyone's attention.

Chapter 23
The Best in Britain

AFTER falling asleep on the display table before the winner had been announced, Madam Pom had awoken with a start, her nose twitching vigorously. A familiar scent was wafting around her sensitive nostrils. Strawberries! She was now fully alert.

As always, after a deep sleep, her face was crumpled on one side. The soft tissues of her cheeks had a habit of moulding to the shape of the surface where she slept, and often stayed like that for a good while after.

Unperturbed by that, the Pomeranian set off in the direction of the delicious fragrance of fruit, at a fast trot. It took only minutes for her to find the lovely red jam spilt beneath the chair, round the back of the homemade goods tent.

Madam sniffed and snorted in delight. The delicious, juicy red preserve was like divine nectar to her. Unlike Mrs Pepper, she cared not a jot that oregano blossom had been added to it. She greedily wolfed it down with relish, barely stopping to draw breath.

The effort was exhausting. The proud pedigree had her fill, then fell into a deep contented slumber, face down in the remaining jam, beneath the plastic chair, unnoticed by anyone.

Zizzi, Zanna and Ziggy had now arrived on the scene, along with other hungry wasps, and were joining in the sticky feast around the unfortunate pedigree's jam-covered head. Her loud snoring bothered them very little as they had heard it all before. They tucked into the sweet treat with equal delight.

Moments later, an announcement over the loud speaker jolted Madam awake. She leapt up in panic, knocking over the plastic chair. Had she just heard the winner being announced? She needed to get back to her table. That rosette for *best in show* was hers!

By now, her usual allergic reactions had kicked in. Her cheeks had puffed up, her eyes were red and inflamed, and her breathing had become restricted, so she rasped and snorted for air. Her face was more crumpled than ever, with the jam covering her swollen face from snout to ears. This mattered not to Madam Pom. She had important things to deal with.

She raced back towards the arena, surrounded by a halo of wasps. In doing so, she ran through the children's fun area and that's where the panic began. A little boy screamed in fright and ran to his mother. She turned and screamed too - for coming towards them was a small, but ghastly, red-eyed monster, with a horribly misshapen crimson face. It was snorting loudly and surrounded by wasps.

Panic now set in amongst all the other children present. Tables were upended, dogs barked, babies cried, and well dressing tablets fell to the ground.

Madam Pom heard the eruption of voices and mistook them for wild cheers to celebrate what she assumed was her victory. She decided to perform a lap of honour around the main arena, delighted by the ecstatic reception. The screams of panic increased.

It was Betty Albright who recognised the hideous creature for who it truly was. She glanced down at her bottles and grabbed a large one, labelled *peppermint oil*. She pulled out the cork with her teeth, and doused herself with some of the contents, before racing into the arena, where Madam was still running around, with the swarm of wasps circling her head.

Madam's eyes had by now nearly closed up, blurring her vision completely. She crashed into a table leg and fell over in total disorientation. Betty raised the bottle over the small dog and sprinkled the oil around her. The wasps immediately dispersed, repelled by the strong smell of peppermint, leaving Madam just a snorting, gasping heap on the grass. Betty threw a large tea towel over the Pomeranian and picked her up.

By now, the three different members of the Greenwood family had heard the commotion and had come running to investigate, along with other concerned villagers. Constance Clark was soon on the scene too, medical bag in hand.

After a calming antihistamine injection, followed by a nice, warm soapy wash, Madam was soon sitting on her haunches, lapping cool fresh water from a bowl. The only lasting injury was to her dignity.

However, it was now that she spotted Skip, standing next to Molly, with the rosette still attached to his harness. By Billy's side, stood the guinea pig cage. From inside its confines, Hazel and the other piggies had watched the stricken Pomeranian receiving her medication, and now had a feeling of impending doom. It was too late to warn Skip.

"What is that?" Madam Pom asked him, in a tremulous voice.

"It's an award," said Skip happily. He showed it proudly to Madam Pom.

The piggies, as one, held their breath. They feared for Skip's survival.

"What is it for?" Madam asked, her voice quaking with disbelief.

Skip wagged his tail and announced happily, "It's the top prize!"

Madam Pom could barely form her words. An intense heat was building up inside her like a volcano ready to erupt in molten fury.

"Who won that?" she asked, trying hard to process the awful sight of it on Skip's harness.

Hazel and her family hid their faces, unable to do anything from inside their cage, and barely able to watch the impending disaster unfolding before their eyes.

Skip wagged his tail delightedly. "Why *you* did of course!" he said. "You fell asleep, so I've been carrying it for you till you woke up. Hazel read it to me. It says, *Madam Pom, Best in Britain!*"

The pompous pedigree's expression changed immediately. Her chest swelled with pride as she got to her feet and stood with her nose in the air. "Didn't I tell you it was mine?!" she cried triumphantly.

Skip grinned from ear to ear, as the guinea pigs breathed a huge collective sigh of relief.

Skip, the small, orange dog, was many things – but he was *not* stupid.

Chapter 24
The Factory Farm

THE mother sow watched carefully. Like all pigs, she was clever. Her keen eyes took in the details of daily life in the huge steel factory farm where she had spent her whole life. From within the metal bars which surrounded her, she observed the humans who came and went.

She knew what time the gates clanked open, and when they clanged shut, what time the bright harsh lights would come on for the day, and when they would shut off, leaving only cold darkness.

She knew which of the workers did their jobs well, which ones lacked focus and took shortcuts. Her sharp brain noted it all, for there was little else to do.

Her young piglet nuzzled her through the bars, seeking her warmth and reassurance. The stall containing his mother was not designed for that. It was for efficient feeding, no more.

The mother sow moved the small amount she could, and whispered to the piglet that he should be alert and ready. Today, the plan would work, she felt sure.

She did not know what lay ahead for her young one if the plan did succeed, but it could be no worse than his destiny within the walls around them. She had heard of a better world out there, where mother pigs raised their young in clean straw nests, where they taught their daughters to do the same - a world where pigs roamed free, foraging for acorns and beechnuts in the fresh air, unconfined and content.

A chain of events was on her side that day. A temporary worker was on duty, with a gossiping colleague who left a gate half shut. They were short-staffed, even less care was being taken than usual.

"Go now!" the mother pig had commanded urgently. "Remember what to do, go!"

The piglet did. He had climbed, squeezed, wriggled and scuttled his way past staff looking the other way, through gates left ajar, to the loading bay outside where the mysteries of the outside world waited.

Only once out there, did he think of his mama left behind. He turned back. Too late. The metal doors were now closing. He had his freedom whether he wanted it or not.

In the loading bay, Vincent, the lorry driver, was preparing to set off. Out of the corner of his eye, he spotted the small piglet heading out from the bay, some way in front of him. He knew he should care, but quite frankly, he didn't. At this moment, his head was pounding, and he had quotas to meet. He didn't have time to chase one errant piglet. Instead, he started his engine and began pulling away.

Just for amusement, he turned his wheel and moved his

heavy great truck in the young animal's direction. A satisfying bump beneath the tyres made him grin to himself.

He reached out for his thermos flask, containing the hot sweet tea which made the long journeys bearable. He cursed at finding it not there, pressing down hard on the accelerator in a mighty temper.

The small piglet stared at the crushed metal object, surrounded by steaming hot brown liquid, which the huge truck had just flattened. He sniffed at it with curiosity then trotted off down the road, naturally drawn to the hedgerow in the distance. The metallic sounds and harsh lights of the crowded, fetid factory were left far behind him.

Back in the metal building, the mother pig began to sing a sorrowful tune beneath her breath. The sow in the next stall heard it and picked up the tune, as did her neighbour. Slowly, the singing passed along the whole row of stalls, grew louder, and carried on to the row after that. Before long, it had spread to all the hundreds of stalls in the building. All the captive sows were singing their hearts out, the song echoing around the walls.

The supervisor, in blue overalls, scowled in annoyance. That wretched noise was disturbing the sensors monitoring production. He turned to his colleague, "It's coming from B275 in stall 153 again. That chuffin' pig is a complete nuisance!"

He would make sure it got a place on the next truck heading out of there. Normally, the sows would be kept for as long as they could produce young, but this one could go early – and good riddance to it.

In fact, he decided to book it, and a few others, a place on the last truck leaving late that very afternoon. The man in blue overalls pressed a few keys on the computer keyboard in front of him, changed a few figures on the screen, and clicked *save*. The nuisance sow would be on her way in a few hours, along with the other awkward animals on her row.

It did cross his mind that it was grumpy old Vincent driving the truck that day. He could moan for England, that one. He hated the late shift and would be irritating the life out of everybody as a result.

As predicted, by the time Vincent arrived back for the last drive of the day, he was indeed in a worse mood than ever. He had been stuck in traffic on the Morecaston road and he was very late arriving. He knew his wages would be docked if he did not still make the final drop off, so he insisted that the last consignment of sows was loaded up. The man in the blue overalls was only too happy to oblige. He wanted to see the back of B275.

Chapter 25
The Good Idea

It was late evening. Henry Goodacre was having difficulty concentrating on the highway ahead. He was cycling along the Morecaston road, after a drinking session in *The Withered Oak*. He had been drowning his sorrows after a bruising encounter with the world's most infuriating woman – Mrs Pepper.

He had once been an important voice on the board of governors for Brierley Bramble Junior School, but lately his opinions seemed to count for very little. The new Chair of Governors barely gave him a chance to speak. She had poured scorn on every suggestion he made for fundraising, ignored his questions, and generally enraged him. It was more than a man could take.

As the traffic lights ahead turned to red, Henry slowed down and drew alongside a truck. The faces of numerous pigs gazed back at him through openings in the side. His eyes met those of B275. A brainwave came to him. How would the prim and proper Mrs Pepper like to wake up to a dirty great pig chomping on the roses in her pretty little back garden? The idea filled him with malicious joy.

He wheeled his bike round to the other side of the truck

and approached the driver's window. "Hey," he called, knocking on the glass. "How much for one of your pigs?" he asked the grumpy-faced man behind the wheel.

"What?"

"One of your pigs, mate, how much?"

Vincent, the driver, stared at him in disbelief. "I can't just chuffin' sell yer one! I've got paperwork and numbers and barcodes coming out me chuffin' ears!"

"Really? Don't they ever miscount when they load the truck?" asked Henry. "Perhaps your numbers and barcodes could suffer a little accident," he suggested, indicating the can of fizzy pop balanced on the driver's dashboard. "They could get a little *smudged*, couldn't they?"

"Smudged?" replied Vincent indignantly, "I'm a chuffin' professional! I keep me paperwork nice and clean…"

His lofty words were interrupted by the clutch of twenty pound notes being waved beneath his nose by Henry (who thought any price was worth paying for this brainwave).

The driver stared at the handful of cash, slightly mesmerised. The wages paid by the company were at the lowest rate possible. He was scraping by most weeks, and his car needed taxing.

"All right, all right," he said. "It had better be one nearest the chuffin' doors, I'm already late!"

He leapt down from his cab, and snatched the notes from Henry's hand, before storming round to the back of the truck. There, he wrenched back the huge, stiff bolt holding everything shut. He yanked open a door and pulled down the ramp – all in a perfect temper.

"Come on then, grab hold of the chuffin' thing!"

Henry had taken out the short rope he kept in his saddlebag in case of emergencies, and now hooked it round the neck of B275, who was too startled to resist. He pulled on the rope and led the surprised sow down the ramp. He stood with it as the driver slammed the door shut, before any other pig could move, and shoved back the bolt as quickly as he could. Vincent leapt back in his cab, chuntering beneath his breath the whole time.

After revving the engine furiously, the bad tempered driver roared off, leaving Henry and the pig at the roadside.

Henry looked down at B275, and B275 looked back up at him. Having acted in haste, his judgement impaired by too much ale, he now began to sober up and regret his actions. The pig was much larger than he realised. The idea had been to tie the other end of the rope to his handle bars, so it trotted by his side. The stupidity of that idea was now pretty clear, and he had no plan on what to do instead.

B275, on the other hand, knew exactly what to do. She had had quite enough of human beings, so she leapt forward to take a good bite out of Henry Goodacre's leg.

He leapt back with a scream before her teeth could connect. Panic now set in. He had a wild beast on his hands. "Go on with you!" he shouted, dropping the rope. "Go on and get away from me!"

So B275 did just that. She turned towards the fields and took her first steps towards freedom, shrugging off the loosely tied rope.

Meanwhile, back on the road, the grumpy lorry driver was still chuntering as he drove. His temper was getting worse. He hated this job. His back hurt from sitting down too much and his head throbbed from concentrating on the road. It had been his third run of the day, his arms were aching badly, and he had no idea what he could have for supper.

He reached down to turn up the volume on his radio, losing concentration for long enough not to spot the broken-down vehicle blocking the road, just around the bend. He slammed on his brakes, stopping inches from its back bumper.

The sharp impact loosened the large bolt holding his rear doors shut, (which, In his haste, he had only half pushed back). It now burst open to reveal the sweet freedom of the evening air to the pigs inside.

After an initial period of bewilderment, B895 was the first to react. She saw her chance and took it, leaping down from the back of the lorry in a split second. B963 and B971 soon followed, as did the entire lorryload of pigs.

By the time the driver realised what was going on, they

were running as a large group across the fields, oinking with delight.

B275 heard their calls and dashed across to join them, leaping for joy. The sows were soon having the time of their lives. They had never before felt earth and grass beneath their feet. They had only ever known cold, hard metal with drain holes. They began splashing through streams, gulping down the cool refreshing waters, tearing up chunks of sweet grass, chasing, frolicking and playing.

They were as they should be, clean and free. This was the world they had only heard about, a distant memory recalled by older pigs who had heard of it from their mothers. So, it did exist, and it was wonderful.

The familiar sounds in the distance had reached the ears of the small piglet who had wandered the fields and hedgerows since that morning, unsure of what to do or where to go. He followed the noises as fast as his legs could carry him, scurrying through tall grasses and crops, crossing meadows and paddling through streams till he reached the group of his own kind.

B275 could not believe her eyes when her son appeared, and she felt his full warmth by her side. She raised her head high and began to sing once more, a joyous song this time, one she never thought she would ever sing.

The late evening was turning into darkness. The pigs knew they needed shelter for the night. Instinctively, they headed for the woods.

Chapter 26
Luarna

Hazel awoke to the faint notes of a haunting melody floating upon the night air. She instantly recognised the exquisite notes of Oro's reed pipe, travelling through the stillness.

The night was so close and humid that she was glad of an excuse to leave the soft hay where she slept. She quietly made her way out into the cooler, fresher atmosphere of the garden, slipping out behind the camellia bush with ease, into the night. The darkness held no terrors for her within The Moon Queen's kingdom.

The scent of the pretty white star jasmine filled the air as Hazel gazed down the length of the garden. At the far end of the lawn, Hazel could see the silvery figures of Godfrig, Merriel, Oro and Fion lighting up the darkness, beneath the silver birch tree. They were sitting in a circle by the marble statuette of the Moon Queen, singing along to the tune Oro played.

Hazel made her way down the garden, drawn to the luminous figures, wanting to be as close to them as possible.

She was soon spotted by Godfrig, who called out to her

in his deep, warm voice, "Why Hazel, how good to see you. Come and join us."

"Indeed," added Merriel, "help us celebrate this beautiful night."

Hazel settled on the grass near Merriel's tail. As she listened to the beautiful tones of Oro's music, Hazel noticed a bright object out of the corner of her eye. A silver hare, with long slim limbs, had appeared in the garden. It was sitting on its haunches watching them intently.

When Oro spotted it, his tune ended abruptly. The pipe dropped from his lips, and he stared at the creature, as if in a daze.

Hazel caught the knowing glances being exchanged between Godfrig, Merriel and Fion.

"Go on, Oro," said Fion. "We know you want to go."

Oro gave a sheepish grin in reply and rose up, fluttering his wings. The hare and Oro both melted into the night.

Hazel had watched in fascination, not daring to speak. Merriel noticed her puzzled expression. "That silver hare you saw is the companion of a special someone, very close to Oro's heart."

Godfrig announced, "I think a visit to the woods would be interesting. What do we all say?"

Hazel's heart fluttered. The thought of repeating that long journey in the dark, which she had taken once before, was more than a little daunting. The look on her face said it all.

Fortunately, Godfrig had some words of reassurance. "Fear not, Hazel, I have a new idea for how to get you there this time. I will return shortly." With that, he took orb form and disappeared into the night.

Soon, Godfrig was back. Hazel was alarmed to recognise the creature he had brought with him. For it was none other than Hubin the raven, who had played a rather mean trick on her and Skip during their previous visit to the Ancient Wood. At least he was on his own and not with his equally untrustworthy companion, Corby.

The large, black, glossy raven joined the sprites on the grass, looking at Hazel with a beady eye.

"Your journey will be much quicker this time, my small friend!" smiled Godfrig.

Hazel swallowed hard. It was one thing to travel with her trusted friend, Blake, but the dark trickster, who had given her such a fright in the woods before, was a different prospect altogether. How sad that herons were not night birds.

Godfrig said gently, "Our friend, Hubin, owes you an apology from last time. He's here to repay the debt." He looked sternly at the raven. "Besides, The Sage will have something to say should he choose any devilment this time."

The small guinea pig still sensed an air of mischief about the bird, but she trusted the sprites completely, so held her tongue.

Hazel was helped up on to his back, with a thick twist of vine keeping her secure. After that, she was up in the air, accompanied by all three sprites in orb form. They clearly intended to keep a close eye on Hubin.

In no time at all, they neared the woods of Lundy. It was then that Hazel began to hear an exquisite melody, even more beautiful and haunting than Oro's. The small piggy felt mesmerised by the notes, their sweetness surrounding her and capturing her senses. They made her feel calm and relaxed, almost as if she was returning home from a long journey, as if she had been away and was coming home to where she belonged.

Soothed by the melody, Hazel was less fearful this time of the blackthorn tree, which stood sentry at the edge of the wood, even though Corby, Hubin's usual partner in crime, sat on one of the branches.

The party travelled further into the wood, Hubin flying skilfully through the trees. They travelled to the ancient part, where The Sage himself lived in the equally ancient oak tree.

Upon landing, Godfrig, now back in his usual figure form, helped Hazel out from under the thick twist of vine, and then down to the ground. Fion was back in figure form too, carrying a lantern to light the way. Merriel remained as an orb, as her tail fins did not cope well with the woodland floor.

"We must be quiet, "warned Godfrig.

They made their way to a small clearing, where a luminescent figure sat on a tree trunk, a reed pipe held to her lips. It was from there that the music came.

Hazel saw Oro sitting on a stone nearby, his face equally transfixed.

The music stopped.

The silvery maiden smiled gently, "Are you ready to join me now, Oro?"

The air sprite flew forward to sit alongside her on the log. He lifted his pipe to his lips. The two sprites began to play a duet, the notes danced upon the air like perfect partners, in total harmony.

"That," whispered Godfrig to Hazel, "is Luarna. No one truly knows what she is, whether she is a wood nymph or an air sprite, for she defies explanation. No one truly cares what she is; they just love her. She appears in the Ancient Wood for only fourteen days at a time. Her melodies are all the sweeter for her short stay."

Merriel continued the explanation, "When she leaves us, she becomes invisible to our eyes. Her music plays each creature across the Rainbow Bridge when it is their time to pass. Her gentle tunes carry them along as the weight of this earthly existence leaves them. They drift like smoke on the breeze, light and carefree, as they hear her sweet melodies."

Hazel understood. That was just how she had felt upon hearing the first notes.

Merriel added softly, "Her melodies will have been the last thing your papa heard as he left this realm."

Hazel felt happy tears well up in her eyes at this thought.

"Ha!" interrupted Fion, a little more harshly, "Oro loses his senses each time she appears!"

"Fion," said Merriel laughing, "you are so harsh!"

"Hmmm," returned Fion, "I just don't get smitten so easily."

At that point they were interrupted, for the most surprising group of visitors had just that moment arrived in the woods.

Chapter 27
A Faraway Land

THE animals of the wood were rather alarmed by the sudden appearance of the pink swarm of creatures, whose joyous calls of enjoyment loudly announced their arrival. As the pigs entered the woods, the calm aura of the trees quietened their excitement. The animals began to slow down and snuffle in the earth amongst the twigs and leaves, pushing aside stones and debris with their snouts, foraging for tasty morsels.

It was Godfrig who stepped forward and immediately took charge of the situation. He picked out B275 as the ringleader and spoke calmly to her. She, in turn, called to the others.

By now, The Sage himself had arrived to see what was happening in his wood. He acknowledged Hazel and the sprites, and then introduced himself to the sows, before inviting them to rest and make themselves comfortable.

Eventually, the pigs settled down on the soft woodland floor. Food and refreshments were organised by the sprites, and the pigs began to tell their tale. They took turns to describe the horrors of the dark, cramped and filthy place where they had lived their entire lives. The Sage, alongside Hazel, Godfrig, Merriel and Fion listened to their terrible stories.

"The first thing we must do is give you names," The Sage said gently.

Hazel joined The Sage and the sprites in making suggestions and helping the animals to choose their new identities. B275 liked the name Sorrel, as chosen by The Sage. Hazel suggested Chestnut for her young piglet, who capered around in happiness at having a proper new name. Merriel thought B895 would suit the name, Willow. B963 became Blossom, on the advice of Fion, and B971 was now Rosie, after a discussion with Godfrig. The other pigs were duly renamed too.

To celebrate, the sprites wove leaves and flowers into garlands and placed them around the ears of the pigs to cheer them further.

It was at this point, that Lucim the owl arrived with news. Now, through the darkness, came the sounds of men and flashes of torches crossing the fields towards the woods. The sausage company had heard about the catastrophe on the road, and had sent out a late-night search party. It wanted its pigs back.

A sense of panic broke out. The sows leapt to their feet. Was their new found freedom coming to an end so soon? Were they going back to the hell from where they had come - or worse?

Sorrel looked at The Sage with desperate eyes, "My Sage, when they take us, will you keep my young one for me? He cannot go back there!"

The Sage gazed calmly at her. He put a gentle nut brown hand upon her head and said, "Fear not, my friend Sorrel, just listen and follow the music."

He closed his eyes.

Across the woods. Luarna heard his silent words, but already knew.

She lowered the pipe from her lips and listened intently, to the sounds of men approaching in the distance, and to other sounds, which only she could hear - sounds which travelled across time, across centuries, across deserts and wastelands, across forests and oceans. She listened and, as Oro watched with devoted eyes, raised her pipe to her lips once more.

Her notes echoed through the woods.

The pigs lost their fear, and stopped to sniff the air, enthralled by the beautiful harmonious sounds. They turned to walk in the direction of the music. As they did so, one by one, they began to disappear, as if evaporating from the woodland floor. First Sorrel and Chestnut, closely followed by Willow, Rosie, Blossom and the rest.

Hazel watched in amazement, and could only stare at the empty space where the creatures had sat only moments before.

In a forest far, far away, in a different land and time, a group of wild boars were waiting. As those they were expecting appeared, the leader of the boars stepped forward.

"Welcome, cousins," he said, "Would you care to join us in a nice cool mud bath?"

Once they had got over their initial surprise, the pigs joyfully accepted the boar's invitation and followed after him, trotting happily.

For the first time in their lives, Sorrel, Chestnut, Willow, Rosie, Blossom and their companions saw the sun and felt its warmth upon their backs. They stepped into its bliss and never looked back.

Far, far away, Luarna smiled, and played a tune upon her pipe.

Chapter 28
The Larsen Trap

In a field on the edge of Morecaston, the calls of a magpie filled the air. His calls were urgent, for he sat upon a perch within the confines of a rectangular mesh cage. The contraption was a Larsen trap, and it sat upon the grass at the edge of the field, by the barbed wire fence.

Magus the magpie had heard his calls as he passed by. He flew down to take a closer look. He hopped down onto the grass and looked in at the bird in sympathy.

"Hey, are you okay?"

"No," came the dejected reply. "I've been here in this thing since this morning."

"Let's get you out," said Magus. "I'll take a look and see how it works from above."

"Wait, no don't!" the bird exclaimed.

Too late, as Magus flew up to sit upon the top of the cage, it immediately gave way beneath his feet. He went tumbling down into the depths of the contraption. It snapped shut above his head. He could only look forlornly through the divide at the other bird. Now they were both trapped.

Hazel clung tightly to the back feathers of Blake the heron as she enjoyed yet another journey through the early morning sky.

The Moon Queen had provided a way for Hazel to summon the large, gentle bird whenever she wanted. All Hazel now had to do was to visit the tall, elegant silver birch tree at the bottom of the Bowood garden, place a paw upon its trunk and wish. A message would be relayed via the intricate network of fungi beneath the soil, and Blake would hear it from whichever tree he was near.

The heron would always answer her call within minutes. He would arrive with a thick twist of vine around his neck, ready for her to slip under as she climbed up onto his back.

She had begun to summon him most mornings. It was partly because she enjoyed the exhilarating ride through the fresh air, watching the world below go by, but also because she liked to see him.

How fond she had become of the grey bird who she now

considered a friend. The warmth of his feathers was a place of comfort and security where she felt totally at peace.

Normally a solitary creature, Blake seemed happy to have the company of Hazel, as he sailed through the skies over Brierley Bramble and beyond. He was always mindful of his passenger, keeping his movements calm and steady with her in mind.

Now, as they soared over Lundy Woods, and over the green side of Morecaston, some instinct made Hazel glance down at one particular spot on the edge of a field.

She could see what looked like a long metal cage. How odd for such a thing to be sitting there, out in the open. She called to Blake.

The heron soon made the descent down onto the ground beneath. As he stopped by the cage, Hazel slipped from his back, onto the grass, to take a closer look.

She saw the two magpies trapped inside, and instantly recognised one. "Magus!" she called in surprise.

"Hi, Hazel," the bird replied. "I don't suppose you've got any good ideas for getting me and Larska out of here, have you? We could both do with your help right now!"

He was trying to sound cheerful and upbeat, but Hazel could sense the fear in his voice. Larska, the other magpie, looked too fearful even to speak. Hazel stared in dismay at the two trapped birds.

It was Blake who spoke next, with a voice full of anger, "I cannot believe they are still using these hideous things! Man can think up so many cruel devices for us."

"What is it?" asked Hazel.

"It's a Larsen trap," replied Blake. "Larska here was the bait bird who was put in one half of the trap to attract the attention of another magpie. When Magus heard his calls, and landed on the top of the cage, it opened the trap door to imprison him. I don't think I need to say any more about what the human's intentions were. Many despise magpies."

Hazel swallowed hard. They *had* to get them out.

"There's a catch up on the top," explained Magus in a sad voice. "I can see it from here, but I can't get my beak into the mechanism."

From where she stood on the grass, Hazel could see what he meant. She had no way of getting up there, and was not sure she could do much with the complicated catch, even if she did.

Her desperate thoughts were interrupted by Blake. "I hate to worry you all," he said, "but I think a gamekeeper might be coming to check the trap. There's a man two fields away heading in this direction, with a shotgun under his arm. We need to act quickly."

With that, Blake flapped his wings and disappeared back up in to the sky, flying in the direction of Lundy Woods.

Hazel looked bleakly at Magus and Larska. Their feathers appeared so beautiful in the sunlight. They were not simply black and white; they each had a lovely patch of blue on their backs which she had never noticed before. Her heart felt so heavy at the thought of what might happen to them.

In the not too far distance, she could see the man. He was getting closer. She desperately tried to think of some words of comfort for Magus and Larska, but her mouth had gone dry and her mind blank with fear. She could only close her eyes and wish as hard as she could.

A sound made her look up. Blake was back, along with a whole host of magpies.

"Hey, Magus," called one, "what are you doing getting caught out like this?"

Magus brightened immediately at the sight of his friends. Larska too gazed up hopefully at the others of his kind.

"Can you do anything with the catch at the top?" asked Magus.

"No, and time is not on our side," replied one of the magpies, glancing at the approaching gamekeeper, but we know someone who can. We can't get them here in time, so we will take you to them instead. Don't worry, Magus!"

In formation, the magpies lowered themselves to latch onto the cage with their feet. As one, they tried to fly upwards, and take the cage with them.

Hazel held her breath, willing them to be quick. The man with the shotgun was getting closer.

Alas, the cage was just too heavy. It came back down, defeating the magpies with its weight.

The gamekeeper was getting closer still and had noticed the collection of birds around his trap. He began to quicken his pace.

Hazel feared the worst, Blake and the magpies too.

At that moment, a couple of crows arrived on the scene.

"We'll help," said one. "We may have no love for you magpies, but we hate Man much more."

"Yeah, we all hate gamekeepers," added the other.

The crows grabbed the cage with their feet, and flapped their wings. With their greater strength applied, the Larsen trap began to lift upwards, higher and higher, until it was sailing over the head of the astonished gamekeeper. He stood with his mouth open, too taken aback to raise his gun.

As quickly as she could, Hazel resumed her place on Blake's back. The guinea pig and the heron gleefully followed in the wake of the birds, heading for the safety of Lundy Woods.

Chapter 29
Rossi

THE magpies and crows flew high over the tree tops, with Hazel and Blake close behind. When a clearing came into sight, their wings slowed, and they began to descend.

The Larsen trap was carefully lowered to the ground, in the ancient part of the woods where it always felt safest.

As Blake and Hazel landed on the ground next to the rectangular cage, the crows left, one calling, "Good luck!" over his shoulder. That just left the friends of Magus to puzzle over what to do next, alongside the guinea pig and the heron.

"What do we do now, Blake?" asked Hazel.

The heron was about to answer when a noise made them both look up at a branch above their heads. Sitting on it was a barn owl.

"Lucim!" said Blake. "Am I pleased to see you. We have a problem here. Could you consult The Sage?"

"Certainly," came the reply. The owl disappeared amongst the trees.

Hazel remembered the owl from her last visit to Lundy. She remembered how she had led the way for them to find

Betty and Madam Pom when they were lost, deep in the woods.

Blake told the other magpies to go for the time being, as their friend, Magus, was in good hands.

After some time, a familiar voice sounded, "Hazel! Blake!" It was Godfrig, the earth sprite, striding towards them with a grin on his face. He was accompanied by a brown rat, wearing a hat and scarf.

Hazel did not know what to be more surprised at: Godfrig appearing in daylight hours, or the fact that he walked next to a rat wearing items of clothing.

"The Sage summoned me," announced Godfrig, in answer to the startled look on Hazel's face. "Only with his permission can I appear in the hours of light."

He then turned to his companion. "This is Rossi, who has come to deal with the lock on that ghastly trap."

"Pleased to meet yers," said the rat in a gruff voice. He made his way over to the Larsen trap. "Hello, gents," he said to the magpies inside, before climbing up the side of the cage, and examining the catch holding it shut.

Rossi sucked air through his front teeth, "Ooh, this is going to need a lot doin'," he pronounced. "It'll take some time and it won't be chuffin' cheap."

"Rossi!" said Godfrig sternly. "None of your nonsense now. Get on with the job please, and mind your language too."

"Heh, heh, all right guvnor, you've got me rumbled there," he chortled. "Let's have a little look."

As he worked, Godfrig explained quietly to Hazel and Blake that the wily old rat had picked up bad habits in his youth. He had been born under *J. Wayne's Service Station* in Morecaston, where his main diet had been discarded takeaway food. He had absorbed the conversational habits of the mechanics working overhead.

Unfortunately, a large rat population had eventually built up under the service station, and pest control were called in. Rossi had had to flee for his life, before finding a new home in the woods. The cap and scarf were doll's items he had picked up on his travels, and now wore all the time, regardless of the weather.

"I've cleaned me act up now, guv," he liked to say to Godfrig, in his deep rusty voice.

The rat's deft paws worked quickly. In no time at all, the rodent had released the mechanism holding Magus and Larska inside.

As the two magpies flapped free, and rattled out their thanks, Rossi sat back on his haunches, with his paws on his hips, and patted the Larsen trap affectionately. "Nice little number that," he said admiringly. "It had a right neat little spring action."

"Good work, Rossi," said Godfrig smiling. "Thank you for your services. I'll ensure some tasty morsels come your way tonight."

"Lovely, guvnor, see you around!" said the rat cheerfully. He raised his hat slightly with one paw, as a parting gesture to Hazel and Blake.

With that, the guinea pig and the heron watched Rossi turn and lope away on his flat feet, his thick tail held out straight behind him.

They expressed their heartfelt thanks to Godfrig, and were about to take their leave, when Lucim the owl appeared once more in the tree overhead. This time, she was extremely agitated. "Godfrig!" she screeched, "It has happened again!"

The look on Godfrig's face was enough to tell Hazel and Blake that something truly serious indeed had occurred. The earth sprite's face darkened with anger and his eyes blazed with fury, as he listened to what Lucim the barn owl had to report.

Hazel was too afraid to speak, for the emotion on Godfrig's face was so intense. It was Blake who asked, "Godfrig, can we be of assistance?"

The earth sprite looked at the heron sadly and explained, "There has been a series of thefts from our world, Blake, thefts which have rocked us all." Godfrig paused to gather his thoughts, and explain as best he could.

He continued, "It has been happening since late spring. We are all used to Man's cruelty and thoughtlessness, but these crimes target those creatures we cherish the most.

They are the ones we fear losing completely from this world."

He stopped and swallowed. "We must go to The Sage now and tell him, without further delay. Come, Lucim."

Hazel and Blake followed in the wake of Godfrig and the barn owl, desperate to know more.

Chapter 30
The Gloved Hand

By the growing light of dawn, way back at the tail end of spring, a dark figure had watched through a pair of binoculars, and waited.

It waited until the red kite had left his nest to hunt for food. Then, it moved, swiftly and with purpose.

It moved towards the group of tall larch trees whose branches swayed gently in the breeze of the early morning. Without hesitation, the figure climbed the first tree, finding footholds with ease as if stepping onto the rungs of a ladder.

It was making its way towards the untidy nest of sheep's wool, twigs and leaves which had sat undisturbed in a crook of the tall tree - until now.

At the noise of the approaching figure, the female red kite left her nest, calling in alarm to her mate.

Nestled in the sheep's wool, was a clutch of three white eggs with soft brown speckles, still warm from their mother's body. A gloved hand reached out and felt for the precious objects. Its fingers closed around one, and swiftly removed it in a single fluid movement. The egg was carefully wrapped and placed into a bag slung across the figure's body.

The process was repeated until the nest lay empty and

bare. With the mission complete, the figure made its way back down the tree.

A car engine sounded, and the figure was gone.

As the car disappeared into the distance, the mourning cries of the red kites echoed through the hills.

Chapter 31
Another Treasure

In a dimly lit room, the eggs of the red kite now lay on a preparation table, where pins, sharp-pointed tweezers, glass jars and balls of cotton wool sat next to a sand tray, a blow pipe and a tiny drill. A smell of chemicals lingered in the air.

The room was a small natural history museum in its own right. On one wall, further treasures were displayed in glass frames. Butterflies from red admiral, and peacock, to small tortoiseshell, were preserved for eternity with their pretty, delicate wings outspread, as if sitting on a leaf. Labels with neat copperplate handwriting noted the specimen's date and location of capture.

On the other side of the room, polished mahogany cabinets stored hundreds of glass-fronted drawers. These housed the more important assets. The large blue and the heath fritillary butterflies, plus the silver-striped hawk-moth were carefully stored away to preserve their value.

So were many hundreds of eggs, taken from the rarest of birds: osprey and goshawk, capercaillie and purple sandpiper, to name but a few.

It was a crime scene where exquisite treasures, stolen

from Nature, were kept hidden away for the secret enjoyment of one individual.

It was crammed full, but the collector always wanted more. There could never be an end point.

In the low light, a man sat staring intently at a computer.

On the screen was the attractive image of a hedgehog. The caption above was less appealing: *Is one of our favourite garden animals facing extinction?*

The facts were laid out: modern fenced-in gardens limited the breeding of hedgehogs and reduced their ability to roam ... they were poisoned by slug pellets ... injured by garden strimmers ... run over on the roads ... The article emphasised how precious hedgehogs were, and how they might just disappear forever if Man did not do more to help them.

It was a sad article, but not to the eyes now poring over it. The word 'precious' carried great meaning. The rarer an animal became, the more appeal it had. The higher its value, the greater was its prize. Perhaps it was time to add a further treasure to the collection.

Another search term was typed in: taxidermy services.

Chapter 32
The Sage Speaks

THE Sage stood beneath the branches of the ancient oak tree, and addressed the assembled creatures of the wood. Amongst them were kings and queens of the fairy kingdoms, and chiefs of the birds and animals. All had gathered to hear the latest tragic news.

Listening too were Hazel and Blake who stood alongside Godfrig, Merriel, Fion and Oro. The Moon Queen herself was sitting with other rulers of importance.

"This time," announced The Sage, his warm deep voice full of pain, "it is a pair of nightjars who have lost all that is precious to them. Their eggs were stolen from their nest in the early hours of this morning."

Those listening to his grave words bowed their heads in sorrow.

The ancient gnome continued, "I was first visited in the spring by those from the red kite community, who came to tell how their young had been removed by a member of Mankind. Reports then came to me of nightingales and hawfinches who lost their young weeks later. Their futures had been stolen by the same thief."

All listened in heavy silence.

The anger was plain in The Sage's voice as he announced, "We have yet to identify the individual, so we must be alert, and on our guard, until we do."

He sighed deeply, his anguish evident for all to see.

"We can never wound Man in the way that he wounds us, but neither can we forgive or forget this hurt. Our friends who have suffered such loss have all done so because their numbers are now so few. Indeed, they are on the verge of being lost from this planet for all time."

The Sage gazed at those who listened to his words, and knew they felt as he did. He went on to say, "To us, they are priceless members of our world, whom we cannot bear to lose, but to some of humankind, they carry financial profit and therein lies the problem."

He took in a deep breath, before ending his speech, "These actions must be stopped, one way or another."

Chapter 33
Edrik the Wanderer

Edrik the hedgehog loved adventure, and Brierley Bramble was the perfect place for this wanderer to spend his days. The villagers knew the importance of holes to connect their gardens. Every fence and wall had openings to create the essential network of routes so necessary to the survival of hedgehogs. Even the ponds had escape ladders, so Edrik and his kind could enjoy a swim without coming to harm. In many gardens, a saucer of meaty cat food or a tray of semi moist hedgehog pellets would be provided overnight, as was a bowl of fresh clean water - never the dreaded bread and milk which would upset his stomach so badly.

Once the daylight dimmed and human activity reduced, Edrik would wander through the lanes and gardens of the village, taking life as it came. He would choose whichever route took his fancy that evening. He knew which gardens had the best food and where the cosiest nesting sites lay. Sometimes he would occupy one of the special wooden hedgehog houses often provided. At other times he would simply curl up beneath a large, deep pile of leaves and sleep snugly.

One of Edrik's favourite stops was the garden of Bowood. John and Billy Greenwood had constructed a purpose-built wooden hedgehog house and a separate feeding station. Both had heavy lids to keep out badgers and foxes. Cat-proof internal corridors prevented the likes of Bruce the tomcat from squeezing his way in and gobbling up any food. Both were situated in a quiet corner of the garden, beneath a cherry tree. The leaves provided perfect bedding, whilst the fallen fruit made a lovely snack.

Occasionally, the guinea pigs would come across Edrik as night fell. They loved to hear his tales of life on the open road. He was a colourful character with great stories to tell and adventures to recount.

He was a particular favourite of Godfrig's. The earth sprite loved the free spirit of the happy-go-lucky hedgehog, often saving him tasty morsels just to hear his wonderful stories.

On this particular evening, as Edrik was on his travels, he came across a new hole he had not seen before. Ever one for a new experience, he ventured through the opening. A strong smell of hedgehog pellets caught his sensitive nose. He was rather peckish after a long night on the road, so he headed straight for the source of the delicious aroma.

A saucer full of food filled his belly, setting him up nicely for a sleep. Fortunately, a hedgehog house had also been provided. Edrik crept in for a look to find brown leaves and hay already lining the space inside.

He usually preferred to find his own bedding, but tonight he was tired, and the rain had started to fall. One thing he hated was getting wet, so he curled up in a ball and closed his eyes, satisfied and content in the dry, warm space.

What he did not see was the infrared camera recording his every move.

If only he knew, he had just walked right into a trap.

Chapter 34
The Trap

A SENSOR sounded an alert. The live feed from the interior of the hedgehog box gave all the information required to the eyes watching it.

Slipping on a pair of thick, black gloves, and picking up a wire cage, the figure opened the door and shone a powerful torch over the dark garden.

Edrik was a heavy sleeper who did not disturb easily, but tonight some sixth sense made him open his eyes. A feeling of unease crept over him. He sat up and sniffed the air. The unmistakable smell of human was becoming stronger – stronger than he liked. Next came the sound of footsteps on the grass, too quiet for the human ear to detect, but not that of a creature whose very survival depended on being alert to predators.

The hedgehog moved to the entrance of the box and sat poised for flight. He needed to work out which direction danger lay in before he made his move. The footsteps were close, the scent of human overpowering. Edrik froze, consumed by fear.

The lid of the hedgehog box began to lift. Edrik knew he had to act now. He leapt from the entrance of the box, and over the human foot which blocked his way. To his horror, he slammed into cold metal. Some sort of cage had been waiting for him, and he had run straight inside.

Edrik turned around quicker than even he knew he could and headed in the opposite direction. This time, he came face to face with the trunk of a laburnum tree. His head was in a spin, but he remembered a cousin who boasted to him about climbing trees. If ever there was a time to find out if a hedgehog could indeed do such a thing, it was now.

Edrik shot out two trembling paws and grasped the rough bark in his claws. He pulled with all his might and pushed off the ground with his back feet. It worked. Edrik had a good hold of the tree trunk, and began working his way up, higher and higher, grasping the surface and pushing his small body up, up to the canopy of the leaves where a fork in the branches led to a nice thick bough.

The hedgehog gasped with the effort, breathing heavily. As his heart slowed down to a more natural rhythm, Edrik had time to think. He was proud of himself and wondered, fleetingly, why he had never done that before. The answer soon came to him – hedgehogs could indeed climb up trees, but rarely did so – because they could not climb back down again.

The torch beam soon picked up Edrik's location. The laburnum tree was not particularly tall. The poor hedgehog could do no more than wait in despair as a pair of black gloved hands reached up to where he sat, and closed around him.

Chapter 35
Dancing Into Danger

A<small>T</small> Brierley Bramble Junior School, the year 5 class were sitting on the carpet, watching Miss Robinson as she produced a box and some small slips of paper.

"Children, we need to decide whose turn it is to bring their small pet into school this week," she announced.

The children looked around at each other as if waiting for someone to speak. It was Louise Little's hand that shot in the air. "Miss Robinson, we all want the singing guinea pig back!"

"Really?" asked Miss Robinson.

"Yes!" cried the class in unison.

And so it was decided that Billy would bring his pets back the very next day for a return visit.

When it became clear that the family of guinea pigs was to spend the day at Billy's school once more, Piggy Mama and Little Rufus were not best pleased. They had not enjoyed dodging all the curious fingers which had poked through the bars of the cage, nor had they particularly liked being stared at by many faces at one time.

Alfie, however, had found the whole thing an adventure, especially the daring trip he and his sister had made to the Head's office.

Hazel was jubilant. A thought had planted itself in her mind, and it was growing stronger each day. Mrs Pepper made a big point of telling everyone she never touched any technology, yet Hazel and Alfie knew different. During their visit to Mrs Kinder's office, they had watched her take a secret smartphone from her large, black handbag and use it quite easily. Why would she do that? The only answer could be that she had something to hide, and Hazel was determined to find out what it was. She just needed a closer look at that phone.

The very next morning, Hazel and family were carried into the classroom by Billy, to squeals of delight from the other children.

"Hey, the rabbits!" called Gemma Peacock, clapping her hands in excitement.

"Will the hamster sing again?!" yelled Tommy Taylor, as he came charging over from the back of the room, as did others who then pushed and shoved to get a better look.

"She's a guinea pig!" corrected Ella Paterson, the sensible girl in the class, "And no, she won't, if you frighten her by shouting and crowding round the cage!"

Hazel was glad the nice girl had spoken up as quickly as she did. She sensed Billy had been about to get rather angry and say it much less politely.

"Quite right, Ella" said Miss Robinson briskly. "Now, let's return to our seats, children. We must take the register and dinner orders quickly as it's assembly soon."

The morning's business was completed in the end, although two recounts were required for the dinner numbers, as two different children forgot to put their hands up for packed lunch or school dinner. They were too busy gazing at the guinea pig who might sing.

Finally, the children were lined up, warned to be quiet (especially as Mrs Pepper was on the prowl again) and led out in single file on their way to the hall.

Hazel had been itching to explore from the moment they had arrived. She was too impatient to leave it till playtime. Much against Mama's wishes, she undid the catch on the carry cage and let herself out. She was closely followed by Alfie, despite Mama's protests.

Once out of the classroom, the two piggies scuttled along the corridor, past the open doorway of the school secretary's office. The lady herself was busily tucking into a couple of digestives and a nice, hot cup of tea whilst she had some peace, and so remained blissfully unaware of their presence. The brother and sister slipped past and into Mrs Kinder's office.

Fortunately, it was empty. Unfortunately, there was absolutely no sign of the big, black handbag in which Mrs Pepper carried her secret phone. Hazel and Alfie could only sit beneath a chair, flat with disappointment, and consider their next move.

As they did so, the strident strains of a piano drifted into the room. Children's voices soon joined it in chorus, singing a cheery ditty with enthusiasm. It was quite an infectious tune about 'lovely food' and the 'lunchtime queue'. Its bouncy rhythm appealed to Hazel instantly. Almost without thinking, she stood on her back legs and began to sway along in time to the melody.

Alfie had watched her in surprise at first, but soon found himself tapping along with a paw to the same rhythm.

Hazel could hold back no more. She began to dance, twirling and spinning across the carpet, lost in the happiness of the moment. Alfie sat with his mouth open, hardly able to believe what he was seeing.

Hazel carried on, whirling and swirling, till she finished in a full pirouette. It was quite a thing of beauty. Alfie clapped his paws together in approval. He was immensely impressed by his sister.

So was Mrs Pepper, who now stood in the doorway.

Both guinea pigs froze in horror as she walked into the room. Before they had time to react, Mrs Pepper reached down and scooped Hazel up in her hand. Her large, black handbag was over one arm. She deftly opened the clasp with her free hand, and popped the small guinea pig in before she had the chance to wheek for help.

Mrs Pepper snapped the handbag shut and left the office. She walked out of the building and crossed the tarmac outside, to where her car sat. She opened the boot and placed the handbag inside. She then smoothed her dress, practised her smile and calmly returned to the school building.

Back in the office, Alfie was left reeling with shock. He had to force himself to run back to the classroom and alert Mama and Little Rufus. Upon arrival, he could barely speak.

When he did finally manage to blurt it all out, neither Piggy Mama nor Little Rufus could believe their ears.

The Chair of Governors had just kidnapped Hazel.

Chapter 36
The Car Journey

Hazel remained cooped up inside the handbag for what seemed like hours. She was hungry and thirsty, not to mention plain uncomfortable. Thankfully, it was a cool rainy day, so heat was not a problem. Hazel sat listening to the faint sound of raindrops hitting the car. It eventually sent her to sleep.

Sometime later, the guinea pig was awoken by sudden noises. She heard a door open, and the engine start up. The car pulled out of the car park, and a short journey followed. It ended minutes later.

Hazel held her breath. What did Mrs Pepper want with her? Would she ever get out of this alive?

After the boot catch sounded, the handbag was opened to reveal the sour expression of Mrs Pepper. Hazel squinted in the light after being trapped in the dark for so long. To her dismay, she was grabbed once more.

This time, the Chair of Governors had taken the precaution of donning a pair of gloves, in case Hazel tried to take a bite out of her fingers, which she certainly felt like doing.

The small guinea pig was now transferred to a metal wire

cage. This was placed on the back seat of Mrs Pepper's car and covered in a blanket. A carrot had been placed in the cage, along with a handful of grass, so at least Mrs Pepper intended to keep her alive for now. That was some relief.

Again, the car engine sounded. They were on the move once more. This time, the journey was a longer one.

After a few miles, the car stopped. Hazel could hear the sound of a door opening, and someone getting into the passenger seat. "Hello, Mum," said a familiar voice.

Hazel was taken aback. Surely, she was mistaken. It couldn't be. She listened for the voice again.

"Have you thought any more about what I said?" asked the voice.

Hazel managed to push a paw through a gap in the wire cage, and lift the edge of the blanket covering it, before peeking out.

It was Priscilla.

She was the daughter of Mrs Pepper? This new information struck Hazel like a thunderbolt, and took all other thoughts from her mind. She listened carefully to the conversation, trying to find out what she could.

"Darling," replied Mrs Pepper, "You know the answer hasn't changed."

"Why not?" came the reply. Priscilla seemed on the verge of tears. "Mum, I want to live with you. Dad's always at work. He never has time for me."

"He works hard, darling, to earn money, so he can look after you."

"Well, I'm lonely, Mum. I'd rather live with you and Cecil.

"No, Priscilla," came the firm reply. "This is not up for discussion."

Mrs Pepper tried to change the subject.

"Anyway, how's school? Are you still friends with that Greenwood girl?"

"You mean the one you call Carrot Top?" came the indignant reply.

"Tut, Priscilla, I called her that once for a small joke!"

Hazel reeled at this second thunderbolt. Had Mrs Pepper really started all the nasty petty *carrot* insults? The guinea pig's mind raced. Now she came to think of it, the regular horrid comments about Molly Greenwood had begun after Mrs Pepper and her husband came to live in the village.

It was all starting to make some sense. Hazel knew the Chair of Governors did not like the Greenwoods. She disliked Billy for his poor test scores and awkward behaviour, and Mr Greenwood had shown her up at the litter pick, which Molly had been at too. The campaign of hate had effectively brought misery to the whole family.

Of course, no one would ever suspect it was Mrs Pepper, because she always claimed she hated technology – yet she had that secret smartphone which she carried in her handbag – how clever.

Now Hazel was more determined than ever to escape and tell everyone the truth, but how?

The car stopped. From what Hazel now heard, they had arrived in the town of Morecaston, where Priscilla and her mother were about to visit a café. Good, that would give her time to think.

As the car doors opened and then shut, Hazel was left with peace and quiet to plan her escape. If only she could find a way out of the cage. She pushed against the door. To her amazement, it swung open easily. In her haste, Mrs Pepper had forgotten to apply the catch properly. Hazel wheeked out loud in happiness at this piece of good fortune. Was this a good omen? Would she now be able to think of what to do next?

She glanced around the car. Was there an open window? No. Were the doors shut properly? Yes. It then dawned on her. There was little point in escaping from the car. She was somewhere in the middle of Morecaston. What would she do if she did get out?

Her eyes then fell upon Priscilla's school bag in the footwell. A mad idea was forming in her mind, the only one Hazel's poor tired brain could come up with. At least it would buy her some time, and get her away from the clutches of Mrs Pepper.

Hazel pulled up the main zipper, and climbed inside the bag. She closed the fastening shut once more behind her, curled up on an exercise book, and rested her head against a fluffy pencil case. Her intention was to keep thinking, but unable to keep her eyes open, Hazel fell into an exhausted sleep.

Sometime later, Hazel was rudely awoken by the return of Priscilla and Mrs Pepper. To her horror, she felt the schoolbag rise sharply up into the air. It came crashing down again as Priscilla flung it onto the backseat.

Hazel let out an involuntary *wheek!* as the bag landed.

"What was that, Mum?" asked Priscilla. "Did you hear it?"

Hazel held her breath.

"Don't worry," replied her mother, telling a lie with total ease, "I've got one of the school's pet guinea pigs on the back seat. They needed someone to take it home for the night."

"Oh," said Priscilla, sighing with relief. She was too eager to get back on her phone to care about some small creature, so accepted the story quite happily.

Inside the bag, Hazel too let out a huge sigh of relief. She just had to sit tight now and think through her next steps.

Chapter 37
A Cruel Decision

THE schoolbag, in which Hazel had hidden, was now sitting on the bed in Priscilla's bedroom. Hazel had braced herself for another rough landing once more. Priscilla seemed to enjoy flinging the bag about.

Hazel watched her movements carefully through an open part of the zip. She was sitting at a dressing table, practising hairstyles in the mirror. With each different style, she would stop and take a photo of herself.

Her efforts were interrupted when her father called to her from downstairs, "Dinner's ready!" to which he added, "And leave that wretched phone up there so you can concentrate on eating for once!"

Priscilla threw her handset onto the bed in annoyance before leaving the room to go downstairs.

Hazel now had a chance to assess the situation. She emerged from the schoolbag and tried to think. She looked at the phone lying there on the bed.

She knew how to use a mobile, thanks to all the practice she had had with Molly's. Then what? Send a text? Tell Molly she had been kidnapped? That was beyond what she could do. She could only type her name, and that took much concentration. Yet, what else could she do? if ever there was a time to try, this was it. Some inspiration would come.

She reached out to the phone. Thankfully, Priscilla, in her haste, had left the phone screen open, with all the icons still visible.

Now what should she do? She looked at the icons on the screen. The first one she spotted was for the *AskMe* app. A thought came to her. Molly would be on that this evening – she always checked it, without fail. Hazel pressed her paw on the icon to bring up the app.

When it appeared, she was in for another shock.

Hazel stared at the screen in disbelief. A post had been drafted, but not yet sent.

Why doesn't anyone want to date Molly Greenwood? 'Cos boys hate vegetables!

Hazel was stunned. This was the girl who had been in Molly's bedroom only the other evening. She was supposed to be her best friend. So *Priscilla* was the one posting malicious comments, not Mrs Pepper!

Hazel realised she had the perfect chance to help Molly, and to stop the nasty abuse once and for all.

It reminded Hazel of a film she had once watched on the TV in Molly's bedroom, during one of her secret visits. In the film, someone was making life miserable for a teenage girl, with vicious online comments. The victim's younger brother worked out that it was a schoolfriend posting the insults, and exposed the guilty culprit. He had found the friend's phone at a party, copied the abuse from the screen, and messaged it to all who knew her. The secret bully was humiliated in front of everyone there at the party.

Hazel could now do the same for Molly.

She had watched Molly on her phone many, many times.

She had also listened with interest when Molly taught her father how to 'take a screenshot' and 'share' it. Like many who had not grown up with technology, John Greenwood had had to take instruction from a member of the younger generation, and had not found it easy. Molly had to take him through it a few times, and Hazel's keen brain had absorbed the lesson too.

First, she needed evidence of the *AskMe* posts made on Priscilla's phone. Hazel knew she had to press two buttons simultaneously. She had a go. Like poor Mr Greenwood, she found this rather tricky, taking countless attempts until, finally, she succeeded, and the screen flashed. The phone now offered three options: save, edit or share. Share was the one. Hazel selected it.

Now Hazel had to find the *Morecaston High School group* in Priscilla's list of contacts, just as it was in Molly's. How she wished she knew her alphabet as she scrolled up and down, searching for the right letters. She made a mental note to learn it at a later date.

If only she could find it. All Hazel would then have to do was post the screenshot, and Priscilla would be exposed for who she really was. She stopped.

There were footsteps on the stairs.

Had she really taken that long? Hazel was furious with herself. Her chance was gone, for now. She quickly pressed cancel in case Priscilla saw what was on the screen. At least she now knew what to do and would be quicker next time. Hazel dashed back over to the schoolbag and climbed in.

Priscilla was soon at her dressing table once more, phone in hand. She tried another hairstyle, and then opened up a box of makeup.

She began applying foundation, followed by eyeshadow

and mascara. She was concentrating hard like an artist at work. Each brush stroke was carefully applied, and the effects considered. When she was finally done, Priscilla picked up her phone and began taking pictures of herself once more.

Each time she would pout and look up at the phone from under her eyelashes, first from one angle and then another. The resulting shot would be examined closely. Then deleted. Priscilla did not like what she saw.

The process happened again and again: pose - click - check - delete. It became quite desperate. Priscilla had to stop as her eyes filled with tears of frustration.

She moved to her dressing table and started her make up all over again. Fresh foundation, new eyeshadow, a different shade of lipstick, her hair completely restyled.

Then it all began again: pose – click – check- delete, pose – click – check- delete.

Hazel had been watching all this from her hiding place. She had burned with rage at this girl for what she had been doing to Molly behind her back. Now, she began to pity her. There was such despair behind the endless 'selfies'.

Priscilla stopped and threw her phone onto the bed in a temper. She grabbed a wet wipe and began scrubbing at her face. "Why are you such an ugly pig?" she shouted at the mirror. "Why does carrot top Greenwood have to have it all?"

She turned and snatched her phone off the bed again and began to type: *How long does Molly Greenwood spend doing her makeup? Not long enough!*

She threw the phone down once more. Hazel watched as the girl sobbed into her pillow, her words muffled, but clear enough to hear, "Stupid carrot top! Daddy's princess! Why should *you* get all the love and attention?! Why don't I?"

So, there was the motive, Priscilla was jealous and insecure. In Priscilla's eyes, Molly was prettier, and her father loved her more. It was pure nonsense, yet it was enough to set Molly up as a target for Priscilla's spiteful envy.

Hazel could still retrieve that screenshot and send the message. That would put a stop to this once and for all. The phone was so close to her hiding place on the bed, and Priscilla's face was buried in her pillow. Her chance was now.

The guinea pig climbed out of the bag once more. Her heart was pounding so loudly against her ribs, she feared Priscilla would hear it. She stretched out a paw to begin again what she had started before. She stopped, paw in mid-air. Hazel could not bring herself to do it.

She now felt desperately sorry for Priscilla, despite what the girl had done. Hazel thought of the wasps, how they had been driven away by Man so often it soured them and made them mean. She thought of The Sun Queen, so insecure that she had to belittle The Moon Queen, simply because of an eclipse.

Hazel realised she held this girl's future in her hands. Was she really going to expose her to all her school friends when she was driven by pain, like a wounded animal that bites others because it is hurt? What happened to the bully in the film, after she had been humiliated? Did nobody ever consider that she too was a girl in distress?

A piercing scream shattered her thoughts.

Priscilla was staring at her in horror.

"What is it?" cried Priscilla's father from downstairs.

He came tearing up the staircase, as Priscilla came running down, equally fast.

"A rat!" she screamed. "On my bed!"

"A rat? Are you sure?" he asked nervously. "Okay, fetch one of my golf clubs from the hall."

Priscilla obeyed. Her father slowly began to walk towards her bedroom door, as softly as he could. Taking a huge deep breath, he leapt through the doorway, golf club in hand, like a caveman approaching a sabre-toothed tiger.

"Goodness!" he laughed moments later. "It's a guinea pig!"

"What?" cried Priscilla. "A guinea pig! Where could that have come from?"

Hazel had jumped back into the schoolbag, in a vain attempt to hide herself once more. Her shaking paws had been unable to pull up the zipper. It had stuck fast, leaving her easy to spot.

Priscilla joined her father in the bedroom. "Hang on a minute," she said. "Mum had a guinea pig in the back of the car. It must have escaped from its cage and climbed into my bag!"

Father and daughter dissolved into laughter, whilst Hazel could only watch them with a sinking feeling.

"Get on the phone to her," said Priscilla's father. "Let's pick the poor thing up for now and keep it safe."

He thought he was being kind. Little did he know, as far as Hazel was concerned, he was about to do the cruellest thing in the world.

Chapter 38
Back to Oakfield Lane

M<small>RS</small> Pepper was on the doorstep all too soon, with her cage ready. Hazel was placed inside.

As she was loaded into the car, Mrs Pepper said harshly, "You like escaping, don't you, guinea pig? Well, it won't be happening anymore!" Her words were more for her own benefit, but they sent chills down Hazel's spine as she heard them. The small animal watched as a secure padlock was attached to the cage and shut with a sharp click.

The car ride was agonising. Hazel thought over the evening. How had she messed it all up so badly? How could she have ended up back in the clutches of Mrs Pepper?

Eventually, the journey ended, and her cage was carried through the door of what she knew to be number 12 Oakfield Lane. This was one address she had never wanted to see again as long as she lived. Her memories of the Bray family were all unhappy ones. To make matters worse, Hazel knew Betty was only yards away in the cottage next door, completely unaware of what was happening.

The cage was taken straight up the stairs into a dimly lit room. It was placed on a table and left there before the door was quickly shut. Hazel's stomach began to rumble. She had a feeling supper was not going to be offered.

Hungry and tired, Hazel settled down on the hard floor of the cage to take some rest. She now knew how Magus must have felt in the Larsen trap. Hot tears threatened to spill from her eyes as she thought of how life had come full circle. Betty had rescued her and her family from the garden of this very house. They had been given a wonderful new life, and now she had thrown it all away. She was right back where she had started, alone and afraid. How she missed her family and all at Bowood. Would she ever see them again?

"Hazel!" whispered a voice.

Hazel started and sat up. Where had that come from?

"Hazel, over here!"

The guinea pig tried to look in the direction of the voice. She could just make out a shape inside another cage close by. As her eyes adjusted to the dim light, she recognised the shape. "Edrik!" she exclaimed. "Is that you?"

"Yes, am I glad to see you!" replied the hedgehog.

"But whatever are you doing here?" asked Hazel.

"I got snatched from the garden, and they stuck me in this cage," explained Edrik. "What about you?"

"It's a long story," replied Hazel. "I suspect I'll have time to fill you in later. For now, what is this room? It smells so strange."

"I hate to tell you this, Hazel, but take a look at the walls around you."

For the first time, Hazel really took notice. She peered around to see glass display cases containing butterflies and dragonflies. They were silent and still like the exhibits in a museum she had seen on TV.

"Are they ...?"

"Yes," interrupted Edrik, to save her from having to say it, "they are, and we could be next."

Hazel looked bleakly at Edrik. It would seem they were both in trouble.

The hedgehog explained further, "An unpleasant man comes in and sits at that box over there."

Hazel looked over in the direction indicated and saw a computer.

"He spends hours on it," said Edrik. "He scares me more than most humans. He walks in a strange way and loses his temper easily. He's always slamming around."

The small guinea pig had been too shocked to think clearly when she first arrived in the room. She stared around for further clues. There were other things stored in glass-fronted drawers too. They looked like ... eggs.

Reality hit the guinea pig hard, taking the breath from her body – they were in the house of the egg thief! This was the man who had caused so much misery for so long, stealing the precious young of birds on the edge of extinction. This was the man who had caused such distress to The Sage,

Godfrig and all those of the woodland. All along, it had been Mr Pepper, husband of the Chair of Governors.

They were interrupted at this moment by raised voices from downstairs. They were muffled and unclear, but their volume and tone suggested an argument. Hazel and Edrik strained to hear what was being said, without success.

Despite now fearing for the very survival of both herself and her friend, Hazel's eyes drooped and closed. She was absolutely drained. It had been a very, very long day. The small guinea pig drifted off into an exhausted, fitful sleep.

Hazel awoke with a start.

The harsh sound of a door slamming interrupted her uneasy dreams.

It was the same for Edrik. He too had awoken, and now looked at her through the bars of their cages with bleary eyes.

The voices were close by this time. A woman could be heard through the wall. It seemed that she was in the room next door.

"Cecil, you can't do this!" she was heard to say.

Hazel sat upright and listened carefully. She recognised the voice immediately. It was Mrs Pepper.

A door handle was rattled hard. Mrs Pepper began banging on the door.

"Let me out, Cecil!"

Hazel looked at Edrik. Whatever was going on?

"Cecil, I must insist you let me out!"

Mr Pepper's replies to his wife could not be heard as they were low and indistinct. Their tone however was clearly angry.

Mrs Pepper now sounded resigned to being locked in, "Could I at least have my handbag, please, darling?"

The low response to that sounded even angrier. Hazel could just make out the words, *secret phone... hidden.*

Mrs Pepper's reply was full of shock and surprise, "You've been in my handbag?"

There was a long gap as if the Chair of Governors was considering her response. When it came, her tone was apologetic and somewhat defeated. "I know, darling, I should have been more honest, but I needed to keep in contact with Priscilla."

The reply from her husband was so loud and furious that his words could actually be heard this time. "I allow you to see her once a month! What more do you want?"

"It's not enough," said his wife bleakly.

This was a revelation. The dominant Mrs Pepper was obviously not the boss at home. Her husband, it would appear, was very much the one in charge.

The conversation now took a different turn.

"Cecil, I just can't," Mrs Pepper was heard to say in an animated voice. "You're not being realistic. Eggs are easy. I just pop those in a bag, but a live hawk chick? I just wouldn't know how to handle it!"

Hazel gasped as she heard those words. Surely not. It couldn't be. She looked at Edrik with wide eyes. Was Mrs Pepper an egg thief too?

This would take some thinking about. How could the prim and proper Chair of Governors, in her smart skirts and dresses, possibly climb trees and empty birds' nests. It was beyond belief.

Hazel thought back over the conversations she had overheard in Molly's bedroom. Were there any clues? She closed her eyes to think hard. Then it came to her – the medal, in Priscilla's schoolbag – she said it belonged to her mother. It was for something sporty ... gymnastics! That was it. Mrs Pepper had been a gymnastics champion.

Now it all made sense.

Mr Pepper had a severe limp. He could barely climb the stairs, never mind a tree – but Mrs Pepper could.

She now sounded pleading, "I got you the guinea pig, didn't I, Cecil? Wasn't that enough? I told you; it can dance and sing."

Hazel gasped at this. So that was why she was here!

This latest revelation stunned her. She looked at Edrik, barely able to speak.

The hedgehog gazed back with eyes full of sympathy. "Look at it this way, Hazel," he said gently, "at least that means they want you kept alive."

That was true. Hazel's mind was in a whirl. There had been so much to take in, so many secrets had been revealed tonight. Yet, what could she do with all the answers she now had? She could tell no one, not whilst she was still trapped at number 12, Oakfield Lane.

Chapter 39
The Alarm is Raised

ALFIE, Piggy Mama and Little Rufus were full of despair. Hazel was gone and they needed urgent help to get her back. The Sprites were their only hope.

The wait for nightfall had been unbearable. Now it was here, the piggies were determined to fight their fear of the dark, and to brave the journey down the garden to where the marble statuettes would be found.

Pushing their way past the camellia bush, the three guinea pigs emerged, peering into the night. Once out, they were joined by Skip and Madam Pom. All walked in silence. With hearts pounding in their chests, they made their way down the garden, heading towards the marble statuettes. Piggy Mama led the way, her two young ones close on one side, the two Pomeranians on the other.

The guinea pigs and the dogs came to a halt. Four orbs of light had appeared before them. The lights grew brighter, before turning into the figures of Godfrig, Merriel, Fion and Oro.

"Do you have something to tell us, little ones?" asked Godfrig, his voice full of concern.

Piggy Mama did the talking, with occasional contributions from Alfie. She told the story of the visit to school, and the events in Mrs Kinder's office.

When Hazel's disappearance had been discovered at Brierley Bramble Juniors, Billy had been distraught. The whole school set about searching for the missing guinea pig. Every adult and child in the building joined in, checking beneath tables and chairs, opening cupboards, moving toys and equipment, but without success.

Alfie, Piggy Mama and Little Rufus could only watch in desperation, unable to tell the humans how they were wasting their time.

To the guinea pigs' disgust, Mrs Pepper even took charge of the search. "I fear the small creature has run away," she had eventually announced. "I did think bringing animals into school was a mistake," she told Mrs Kinder with an annoying told-you-so raising of her eyebrows.

John Greenwood was contacted, and Billy was taken home with the three remaining guinea pigs.

The sprites listened patiently to the sad tale. "We had sensed something was wrong," said Merriel. "Your information now confirms what we feared."

"You were right to come to us," said Godfrig. "We know that took courage. You have now played your part and must return inside to rest as best you can. We will take things from here."

The sprites accompanied Hazel's family, Skip and Madam Pom back up the garden, and saw them inside, before taking to the air and heading in the direction of the Ancient Wood.

Chapter 40
Cecil Pepper's Dreadful Evening

As Cecil Pepper sat down to enjoy the large glass of whisky he had just poured for himself, he thought he heard a noise from outside. He put down his newspaper and glass, and went to have a peek through his front window. As he peered out at the dark night sky, he was puzzled. What was that strange, silvery object?

It seemed to be a ball of light floating in the air. Mr Pepper opened his front door for a closer look.

He stepped out of his doorway and into his small front garden. The orb was still some way ahead of him. He approached it slowly, fascinated by its luminous beauty, but puzzled by whatever it could be.

The light shimmered and sparkled before his eyes. It radiated peace and happiness. It made him think of his childhood and of happier times when life was joyful and carefree.

The door to his cottage stood open behind him. In the darkness, two small shapes slipped inside and disappeared up the stairs.

As the ball of light moved, Mr Pepper was drawn to follow, hardly aware of what he was doing. He walked

forward in slow motion, mesmerised, struggling to understand what he was seeing and feeling.

The door to his cottage slammed shut behind him.

He snapped out of his trance immediately. He spun
around and rushed to grab the handle. The door would
not budge. His thoughts raced. He was baffled. The door
had to be physically locked for this to happen. He rattled
the handle once more, but to no avail. He was shut out of
his own home – but how? He pounded on the door with
frustration.

Realising he had to deal with the situation another way,
he turned back to think.

He was in for a much worse shock.

For his small front garden was full. On every surface,
from low wall to tree branch and dustbin lid, sat many,
many silvery birds and insects of every shape and variety.
Around and between them floated more orbs of glimmering
light.

It was quite a spectacular sight, but not one Cecil Pepper
appreciated at all. He was frozen to the spot. What on earth
was happening?

As his panic-stricken eyes darted around, trying to
make sense of it all, it slowly dawned on him that there was
something very strange indeed about the many creatures
in his garden. They were pale and translucent, like ghostly
forms not of this world.

Mr Pepper stared with a dry mouth and a heart beating
ever faster. The orb drew level with his eyes and the silvery
voice of The Moon Queen could be heard. "Cecil Pepper,
what do you see before you?"

With tremendous effort, Mr Pepper held in the scream
building up inside him, but could not prevent a whimper of

fear escaping as he stammered, "W-who are you? W-what do you want?"

"I want you to look and tell me what you see," replied The Moon Queen's voice.

"I-I don't know," said Mr Pepper desperately.

"Then let me help you," she said. "What you see before you is the spirit of each and every creature whose life you stole from us, whilst you plundered our world for your own gain."

Mr Pepper looked aghast at the ghostly shapes around him.

"Cecil Pepper," continued the voice, "you see before you red kites and ospreys, peregrine falcons and buzzards, butterflies and dragonflies ... I need not go on, Cecil Pepper, for you know only too well what creatures might be here. They are all the creatures of beauty who never had their time in the sun - because you robbed them of that."

Mr Pepper shrank back against his doorway, quivering in absolute dread.

"We cannot make you pay the price, Cecil Pepper," said The Moon Queen, "but your own kind can."

At that moment, a strong torch beam interrupted proceedings. It was shining up over Mr Pepper's head, and a human voice now spoke, "Mr Pepper!"

Chapter 41
A Familiar Face

In the darkness of the room, Hazel and Edrik sat miserably in their cages. Neither had been able to think of a plan of escape, no matter how hard they tried. Even rescue seemed unlikely as no one could even know where they were.

Hazel knew that Alfie saw her being snatched by Mrs Pepper, but what good would that do? He could only tell Mama and little Rufus, not the humans. The Greenwoods probably thought she had just escaped from the cage at school and run away, as Mrs Pepper said.

Edrik felt the same – no one could know he too had been seized.

Their thoughts were interrupted by a scratching at the door. As Hazel and Edrik watched, the handle turned slowly but surely, until a click sounded, and the door opened.

Two shapes entered the dark room.

"'Ello again!" said a deep, throaty voice.

Hazel and Edrik both sat up and looked in the direction of the voice. On the floor of the room, Hazel's eyes could just make out the shape of a cat and another shape she recognised immediately – that of a rat wearing a hat and scarf.

"Rossi!" she said in delight. "You've found us! However did you get in here?"

"Heh, heh, I'm a rat! We can get in anywhere," he replied, winking. "I'm here with my good friend, Tabitha," he continued, "who will be assisting us this evening."

Hazel recognised P.C. Frankie's cat. She had helped once before during the rescue from Lundy Woods.

"Glad to see you both!" said Hazel, with great relief.

She and Edrik watched with curiosity as Tabitha jumped up onto the window sill. They didn't ask why she was there, as a plan was clearly being put in place, and that was all they cared about.

In the meantime, Rossi found his way up onto the table top.

Hazel saw the puzzled look on Edrik's face. "Don't worry, Edrik," she said, "This is Rossi, the best locksmith around – he'll soon get us out!"

By now, the rat was up on his hind legs, closely inspecting the locks on the cages that held them both captive.

After a few moments, he pushed up his hat, scratched his head and sucked in air against his teeth. "Well, I'll see what I can do," he announced, "but it ain't gonna be cheap."

"Oh dear," said Edrik, glancing at Hazel in concern.

"Rossi," said Hazel, looking sharply at him with a furrowed brow, "Really? Now of all times?"

"Ha, ha," came the reply, "only kidding! Let's get to work."

Chapter 42
Secret No More

Cᴇᴄɪʟ Pepper was still desperately trying to comprehend what was happening to him this evening.

He was locked outside his own home, surrounded by orbs and ghostly creatures, a voice had spoken to him out of nowhere, and now this.

He finally realised he was face to face with P.C. Frankie and the woman from next door, Betty Albright. At least he was now being addressed by human beings. He glanced around. The orbs and ghostly creatures had gone.

The police officer was staring at him, with a face full of fury. "Mr Pepper, I demand to know why *my* cat is looking at me from *your* upstairs window!"

"What?" shrieked Mr Pepper.

Breathing in, he looked in confusion at P.C. Frankie, who was pointing upwards, his hand shaking with rage. Mr Pepper followed the direction of the policeman's finger, and saw the face of a black and white cat meowing through his upstairs window.

"What the devil?" he protested. "I have no idea how *that* got there!"

"Well, I want *that* back right now!" shouted P.C. Frankie, beside himself with indignation. "Open up your door immediately!"

"I wish I could," retorted Cecil Pepper, "but some creatures have shut me out!"

P.C. Frankie and Betty exchanged glances.

"Are you quite well, Mr Pepper?" asked Betty.

Mr Pepper stared back, unsure of the answer to that after what he had been through.

As no sensible answer was forthcoming, P.C. Frankie lost patience. "Stand to one side, sir!" commanded the police officer. All he cared about was his beloved Tabitha. He pushed past Cecil Pepper and grabbed the handle of the front door.

It swung open with ease.

Cecil Pepper gaped at the doorway, dumbstruck, as the irate policeman raced through the door of his home and up the stairs, closely followed by Betty. The only thing Mr

Pepper could do was limp after them. "You have no right to enter my home!" he protested loudly.

His words fell on deaf ears.

Stairs had always been difficult for Mr Pepper, so by the time he joined them, P.C. Frankie was already standing by Betty's side, cradling Tabitha in his arms and staring in complete revulsion at what was before them. It was a ghastly treasure trove of birds' eggs, butterflies and other insects, all frozen in time and pinned beneath glass.

A loud wheek made Betty and P.C. Frankie look sharply to the side, where their gaze fell upon Hazel the guinea pig and Edrik the hedgehog huddled together beneath a table. Words failed them.

Betty was about to dart forward to pick Hazel up when a loud commotion made them all freeze. A banging sound came from another door on the landing, and a woman's voice began crying out for help.

"Now, hang on ..." Mr Pepper tried to speak, but P.C. Frankie and Betty were in no mood to listen to anything he had to say. They pushed past him once more and rushed to the door.

"It's locked!" yelled P.C. Frankie. "Pepper, get this open *now!*"

Cecil Pepper tried to bluster a defiant reply, but even he could see that any protest was now futile. The game was up.

He sullenly produced a key from his shirt pocket and handed it to the police officer in weary defeat.

The door was hastily unlocked.

It swung open to reveal a dishevelled and weary Mrs Pepper.

Chapter 43
Reunited

Jᴏʜɴ and Billy Greenwood were just stepping out the door of Bowood, ready for a walk with Skip and Madam Pom. It had become a habit to take their exercise in the relative cool of the evening during the hot summer months.

It had also been a way of distracting Billy, for he had cried himself to sleep each night since Hazel's disappearance. John Greenwood himself had felt sad too, as had Molly. They had dreaded telling Betty. They knew she would be devastated, as indeed she was. The small guinea pig was a character they had each become very attached to in their own way.

For John and Billy, the evening walk had also been an escape from Molly and her moods. To their surprise, she now appeared in the doorway, ready to join them. "I could do with some fresh air," she said.

Billy and his father exchanged glances, but agreed as she did not seem in a fighting mood for once. Madam Pom and Skip were overjoyed at having the full family with them on the walk, and both twirled in delight at the sight of her on the step.

As the three members of the Greenwood family strolled

down the dirt track leading from their house, they stopped in surprise. A trail of feathers lay ahead of them. It was quite a deliberate trail, far too neat to be accidental. John, Billy and Molly peered at it, whilst Madam Pom and Skip sniffed at it in curiosity.

The feathers continued down the track, so the Greenwoods, intrigued to say the least, decided to follow their path. The trail took them out along the road at the end. From there, the feathers carried on well into the village, remaining the focus of everyone's attention – until that is, they noticed a rather strange scene outside number 12, Oakfield Lane.

The Greenwoods arrived just in time to see a police van pulling away from the kerb. What they did not see was Cecil Pepper safely locked up in the back.

They could only watch with open mouths as a police car arrived for Mrs Pepper. A sympathetic officer draped a blanket around her shoulders and led her out to sit in the back, before she too was taken away.

"Jim, whatever is going on?" asked John Greenwood as P.C. Frankie came towards him, his precious cat still cradled against his chest.

"It's a long story, John," replied the police officer wearily, "but Betty has some good news for you."

At that, Betty stepped forward and presented Billy with Hazel the guinea pig.

Billy, John and Molly gasped in unison as they saw the

piggy. Tears of joy ran down Billy's cheeks as he took his missing pet gently into his arms and held her close, caressing her ears with a shaking finger. John and Molly beamed with joy, their eyes brimming too at the sight of them reunited.

Once the initial surprise had worn off, John looked to Betty for an explanation, especially as he now noticed a box at her feet. He could see a hedgehog sitting comfortably within the folds of a towel, munching on a selection of plants and herbs.

Betty smiled sadly. "It would be much easier to just show you," she replied quietly. With that, she led John, Molly and Billy into number 12 to see for themselves.

Chapter 44
Sweet Dreams

Bᴀᴄᴋ at Bowood, after a check-up from Constance Clark, the vet, Hazel had been returned to the outhouse, along with a handful of calming herbs and plants supplied by Betty. She was now snuggled up with Piggy Mama, Alfie and Little Rufus, in the warmth and comfort of the upstairs nesting box of the hutch.

Skip had already greeted her earlier in the evening with a small comforting lick on the ear, and – to everyone's astonishment – so had Madam Pom. She later claimed she had only meant to sniff Hazel out of curiosity, but all knew different.

Later that night, as the guinea pigs lay deep in slumber, a small blue orb appeared floating above their heads.

It was only Hazel who awoke to see it, for she sensed its arrival in her dreams.

The gentle voice of Merriel could be heard to say, "Hazel, Her Majesty wants to tell you how pleased she is that you are safely home, indeed we all are. You remain a special individual who we all care about very much."

Hazel smiled, her bright eyes showing her gratitude.

"Yet, Hazel," continued Merriel gently, "we feel something troubles you still."

The water sprite's warm voice was so soft and soothing, that Hazel immediately felt able to open up and explain what it was that still preyed on her mind. She described what had happened in Priscilla's bedroom, how she had intended to gain revenge for Molly, but how in the end, she could not bring herself to complete the plan.

"Did I do the right thing?" asked Hazel. "I feel that I let Molly down."

"No, Hazel," said Merriel, "you did not. You have kind instincts, and you chose the right path. I am proud of you, and The Moon Queen will be too when she hears of this."

The exquisite orb of blue light shimmered in the darkness, as Merriel added, "Worry not, Hazel. I know just how we can sort this out. Luarna will help us. I will ask Oro to call for her with his pipe."

Merriel told Hazel the plan. Hazel gazed gratefully at the orb as she heard the details, and breathed a deep sigh of relief. Her rest that night would now be truly peaceful.

"One last thing, Hazel," said Merriel before she took her leave, "The Moon Queen says we have much to celebrate now. So, be in the garden tomorrow, at midnight, with all the other little ones, for happy times await you, in the Ancient Wood."

The orb melted away, leaving Hazel to close her eyes once more in blissful sleep.

In the darkness of Priscilla's bedroom, a gorgeous silver orb of light appeared. It danced around the room for a few moments before coming to a standstill on Priscilla's pillow.

As the girl slept, her eyelids fluttered. Uncomfortable thoughts filled her dreams with pain and sorrow, and with anger and bitterness. They showed on her face, in the furrows on her forehead and in the lines in her young skin.

The orb began to shimmer, and as it did so, the exquisite melody of a reed pipe could be heard. Its notes floated in the air and surrounded the sleeping Priscilla. They bathed her with warmth and kindness, and replaced her bitter thoughts with sweeter ones. They caressed her cheeks, smoothed out the lines in her face and entered her dreams.

The notes told their own story. They told Priscilla that she was beautiful, they told her she was loved, and they melted away her pain.

When her job was done, Luarna smiled.

The orb shimmered once more before melting away into the night.

Priscilla awoke in the morning with a light happy feeling she did not recognise. Her sleep had been deep and tranquil, leaving her refreshed and at peace with herself.

She noticed her phone and her face fell. She reached for the handset and found the red and blue question mark.

A tap of her fingertip brought the Molly Greenwood thread to the screen. Priscilla's eyes filled with tears as she reread her own hateful words. With her own mind soothed, the anger and hurt in the things she had posted stood out with dreadful starkness.

She began to type.

As the electronic beep of an alarm invaded Molly's sleep, she awoke to face the day. She pulled her phone from beneath her pillow, and tapped the red and blue question mark, the way she usually did.

Her blurry eyes began to scan the screen, ready to deal with the latest abuse with weary acceptance.

Molly sat up, hardly daring to believe her eyes. AskMe had a new post on the thread she visited each day:

Molly, you are a beautiful person who lights up the world. The ugliness was all mine. Forgive me.

Was it a joke? Where was the catch?

She looked again.

The hateful words were gone. All had vanished. There were no more references to carrots, or anything else remotely unpleasant at all. Molly blinked and looked yet again.

It really did seem like the nightmare had ended.

She leapt out of bed, hardly able to think straight. She read the words again and again, until her eyes ached. Crossing to her window, Molly threw it open and gazed out over the garden of Bowood and the meadows beyond. Everything, from the grasses and plants, to the trees and the hedges, was bathed in gorgeous sunshine. Nature seemed brighter and more resplendent than ever. She breathed in the delicious warm air, stretched up her arms, and let out a long luxurious sigh of contentment.

The deep pain which she had felt for so long, began to ease. Scars would remain, she knew that, but for now the day stretched out before her with a welcome kindness that it had lost till this moment.

Molly picked up her phone once more. She wanted Priscilla to hear the good news.

Chapter 45
A Night of Celebration

F<small>OUR</small> red kites soared through the dark night sky in formation. Their magnificent pale grey heads appeared as silhouettes against the moon. Their striking golden eyes searched out their promised destination.

As it came into view, they followed a smooth path to the ground below. The glow from numerous small lanterns and four silvery figures lit their way.

In the garden of Bowood, Hazel and the other animals of the household stood with faces upturned, amazed at the sight of the huge birds making their descent.

Hazel swallowed as she noticed the width of their wingspan, and shot a glance at those beside her. The sprites, as always, remained a calm and steady presence. However, Alfie, Piggy Mama, and Little Rufus looked truly terrified, whilst Madam Pom and Skip appeared ready to run for their lives.

Godfrig was the first to reassure them as the red kites touched down. "Fear not, small ones. These handsome birds are indeed powerful and strong, but they are here as friends and will do you no harm. They are paying their respects. The humans who stole their futures can commit no further crimes. For that they are grateful to us in the natural community."

The piggies did their best to believe him as they gazed at the birds' sharp, black, yellow tipped beaks and ferocious looking talons.

Godfrig turned to the birds and smiled. "Good evening, friends. We are honoured indeed to have your company. I know The Sage has instructed you on what we require."

The red kites nodded politely. The leader, a female kite, responded in a deep, golden voice, "We thank you, Godfrig. We are happy to help."

Despite their grandeur, the large birds followed the instructions now given by the earth sprite. They folded their legs, before lowering their undersides to the grass, and waited patiently.

The rather nervous guinea pigs were each assisted by Godfrig, Merriel, Oro and Fion to climb onto the back of a bird. Once in place, every piggy was held firm and secure within two thick twists of vine.

Final words of reassurance were offered by the sprites,

and then it was time. The red kites stood up, spread their wings and set off for the skies.

Wheeks of excitement filled the air as Alfie, Piggy Mama and Little Rufus experienced the sheer exhilaration of being airborne for the first time in their lives.

Hazel laughed gleefully as she looked across at her family. Her two brothers were watching the world go by with eyes like saucers, loving the thrill of it all, whilst Piggy Mama was clinging on for dear life, her eyes tightly shut.

Their destination was the Ancient Woods of Lundy. A personal invitation had been sent out from none other than The Sage himself, and Hazel was full of anticipation for the evening ahead. As was her family, for none of them had ever been to the woods before, or experienced its enchantment.

Back in the garden, Skip and Madam Pom waited, hardly daring to breathe. Their transport had arrived too.

Four even bigger birds were now standing on the lawn of Bowood, exchanging courteous greetings with Godfrig. They were large, powerful white-tailed eagles, the only birds truly capable of doing what The Sage had requested.

Around their upper bodies were lengthy twists of vine, and attached to the other end, was an object which Hazel would have recognised all too soon, had she been there. It was the Larsen trap from which Magus and Larska had been freed.

It was of rather a different appearance now. The top part had been removed to create an open rectangular container. It had been filled with soft hay, moss, leaves and twigs to create a much more pleasant place for any animal to be.

It was in this that the two Pomeranians were to be transported. Madam Pom and Skip seemed hesitant, until Godfrig gently reminded them, that it was quite a walk to Lundy Woods. At this, Madam Pom leapt forward and allowed herself to be helped inside. Skip soon followed.

After the lengths of vine attached to each corner of the cage had been carefully checked by the sprites, Godfrig gave the command. The eagles began to beat their wings, before rising up into the air. The container followed, the two Pomeranians' faces sticking out over the side, a mixture of fear and excitement In the expressions on their faces.

Oro took flight to follow them, with Godfrig, Merriel and Fion taking orb form to travel alongside him through the midnight air.

The Ancient Wood was alive with celebration. Lights of varying shapes and sizes lit the darkness of the night. Fireflies hovered in and around the trees, keeping the company of orbs and woodland sprites. Whilst Mankind slept, the woods belonged to the creatures of the night, from animals of the wild to those of other realms. The atmosphere was vibrant.

Beneath the branches of the majestic ancient oak, home to The Sage, Ruler of the Woods, were three thrones hewn from oak. On the middle one, sat The Sage himself. On his right, sat The Moon Queen, and on his left, was The

Sun Queen, both guests of honour for the evening. The three monarchs were engaged in pleasant conversation, all previous unpleasantness between the two queens now forgotten. The warm summer night with its heady perfumes and exquisite aromas added to the convivial atmosphere and put all at ease, as they waited for the final guests.

Those guests were arriving now.

Hazel, Alfie, Piggy Mama and Little Rufus descended into the clearing around the oak tree, on the backs of the red kites.

Moments later, they were joined by the sprites and the four white-tailed eagles, who gently lowered down the container with Madam Pom and Skip aboard.

The sprites were soon back in figure form. Once they had paid their respects to the three monarchs, they began helping the animals of Bowood to disembark and join the trio of rulers beneath the tree.

The eagles and the red kites were cordially thanked by The Sage, before they disappeared to join the celebrations elsewhere in the woods.

"Welcome, my small friends," said The Sage, addressing the Bowood animals in his deep, gentle voice. "Hazel, will you introduce me to your companions?"

"Certainly, My Sage," replied the small guinea pig. She did as he asked, introducing Piggy Mama and her brothers, followed by Skip and Madam Pom.

"Actually," announced Madam Pom, unable to contain herself, "my full name is Madam Pom Pom de Belvedere Dancing Queen."

There was silence all around as The Sage gazed at the proud Pomeranian with his velvety nut brown eyes. Madam

Pom looked down at the woodland floor, suddenly realising she had perhaps spoken out of turn.

The Sage smiled, his eyes twinkling as he spoke. "Well, Madam Pom," he said, "it is only right for you to be treated as royalty then. Do come and sit by my feet."

Everyone breathed a huge sigh of relief, especially Madam Pom. The pedigree Pomeranian leapt up and trotted over to the space indicated by The Sage. She settled down, looking thoroughly pleased with herself. Her only regret was that she had not worn her Best in Britain rosette.

The guinea pigs and Skip were invited to make themselves at home too. A soft covering of leaves and moss had been spread around the woodland floor to ensure extra comfort for them. Refreshments of wild herbs, plants and vegetables, washed down by cool, refreshing spring water, were soon served up by Godfrig, Merriel and Fion. Goblets of oakleaf wine were presented to The Sage, The Moon Queen and The Sun Queen.

In the meantime, Oro took his place on a small log placed there for the purpose. He raised his reed pipe to his lips and began to play a tune.

As he did so, a silver hare appeared at the edge of the clearing. Oro's eyes brightened, and the tempo of his tune increased. In no time at all he had been joined on the log by Luarna herself. Their duet sweetened the air and spread a joyful feeling far and wide.

In time, The Sage called all to attention. He raised his goblet and proposed a toast, to remind each and every one of them why they were there. It was to celebrate the recent triumph of good over evil, it was to celebrate the wonders of Mother Nature herself, and it was to celebrate the beautiful summer night of happiness that they enjoyed at this very moment.

And so the festivities truly began. The creatures of the night knew how to have fun. Some frolicked and chased in and around the trees. Others danced in the air, and on the ground, to the cheerful tunes of Oro and Luarna. Laughter and merriment filled the woods. Even The Sage, The Moon Queen and The Sun Queen joined in.

Familiar faces could be seen finding sport and entertainment. Blake the heron sat in a tree, peacefully soaking up the atmosphere in his own quiet way.

Nearby, was Edrik the hedgehog, surrounded by an audience of woodland creatures, thoroughly enjoying his tales of life on the open road.

Elsewhere, Rossi the rat was entertaining his own listeners with some rather saucy service station stories.

In the branches above them, Magus and Larska the magpies were singing exuberantly with their pals.

The piggies and the Pomeranians had never had so much fun. Hazel, Alfie and little Rufus had thoroughly exhausted themselves, as had Madam Pom and Skip. Piggy Mama had watched in delight, often giggling as she had when she was a much younger guinea pig.

As Hazel sat down for a rest to catch her breath, her mind suddenly flashed back to the recent horrors of being trapped in a cage, at the dreaded 12 Oakfield Lane. The feeling was intense, and made her wish for a quiet moment alone.

She slipped out of the clearing, and headed for a dark space beneath a low lying branch. Once there, she closed her eyes and thought about the one who was so often on her mind - Piggy Papa.

For one fleeting moment, she could sense his strong presence. A calming warmth surrounded her and stilled her mind. She could almost smell the muskiness of his fur and feel his breath on her cheek. It was a single moment in time which hung in the air, like a precious jewel, then melted away into the night.

Hazel had no time to reflect further, for a familiar silvery voice sounded nearby. "Hazel?" it called.

The small guinea pig left her hiding place to see none other than The Moon Queen herself standing there. The moonstone atop of her staff glowed with pleasure.

"There you are," said Her Majesty, with a gentle smile. "How nice to see you, Hazel. I hear much has happened since we last met. As usual, you have shown yourself to be brave and determined. I am proud of you."

Hazel blushed with pleasure at the monarch's words, but before she could respond, The Moon Queen spoke again, "I thought you might enjoy the company of a special guest tonight." She stood to one side to reveal a ginger rough-haired guinea pig, looking slightly bewildered.

"*Spikey!*" exclaimed Hazel in surprise.

"*Long-toes!*" cried the ginger piggy.

"However did you get here?" Hazel asked.

"An orb appeared in our cage, and it told me I deserved a night of fun away from Rupert," came the reply. "Can you believe I came here on the back of a big bird?"

"Yes," said Hazel laughing, "I can!"

She smiled gratefully at The Moon Queen. "Thank you, Your Majesty."

The monarch returned the smile. "I will leave you both to enjoy the festivities," she said gently, before turning to walk smoothly away.

Hazel looked cheerfully at the guinea pig. "I never got the chance to ask you your name. I'm Hazel."

"I'm Leo," replied the ginger piggy happily.

"Well, Leo, I'm very pleased to see you again," said Hazel, "Let's go and join the fun."

And that is just what the two piggies did.

Useful Websites for Animal Lovers:

Compassion in World Farming: www.ciwf.org.uk

A wonderful organisation that campaigns to improve the often brutal lives of animals used in food production.

Guinea Pig Magazine: guineapigmagazine.com

Based in the UK, and available across the world, this publication promotes the welfare of piggies in a fun, but informative way. A subscription makes a great gift.

The Guinea Pig Forum: theguineapigforum.co.uk

This is a discussion group run by piggy lovers, who discuss all things related to our small, furry friends – a great place to ask questions and receive advice.

Dogs Trust: dogstrust.org.uk

This canine rescue organisation never puts a healthy dog down. The website is a wonderful source of advice and information on our four-legged friends.

Hedgehog Street: www.hedgehogstreet.org

This website is dedicated to the preservation of hedgehogs, providing information on how to help them, and mapping out where they are in the UK.

Help Wildlife UK: www.helpwildlife.co.uk

A directory of wildlife rescues in Britain, it enables people to seek local assistance for sick or injured wild creatures. The website also contains advice on when and how you should help an animal.

Other countries will have similar organisations.

About The Author

J.P. Stringer is Yorkshire born and bred, now living in Derbyshire. She shares her life with her husband, three children, two dogs and five rescue guinea pigs.

She would *love* to hear from any reader with comments to make on her story!

Please do contact her on: brierleybramble@gmail.com

About The Illustrator

Natasa Devic is a graphic designer and illustrator. Of all the combinations of techniques, she prefers to draw traditional illustrations in pencil. Her love for animals and drawing has grown since she was a child, and she is happy that she managed to combine two loves that are her inexhaustible inspiration. Nature is art in itself, and leaves infinite possibilities for creativity, and she is happy to be able to show that beauty in her own way.

Behance: https://www.behance.net/natasadevic
Fiverr: https://www.fiverr.com/nacika88

A *Huge* Thank You To:

String: for being my editor-in-chief, husband and soulmate, and for doing all the boring stuff around the house, so I can have fun writing.

Robb Stringer: for your technical help and creative input.

Hazel Douglas: for your friendship, your editing, your numerous helpful suggestions and for giving me the confidence to write.

Lizzy & Leo Douglas: for providing inspiration.

Natasa Devic: for your wonderful illustrations which brighten the story and bring the characters to life.

Kim Fowler: for the original character concepts which were too good to change, and for the lovely woodland design at the end of chapter eight.

Adrian Doan Kim: for yet another glorious book cover.

Alison Byford, Rik & Helen Cridland of Guinea Pig Magazine: for your continuing assistance, and for educating the world on how to give piggies the best lives possible.

Kieran (K-dogg) Walker: for all your support from the very beginning and for your meticulous proofreading.

Sharon Hawkins, Donna Tunley, Georgia Leigh, and fellow writer, Fran Worthington: for all your help and encouragement with both Brierley Bramble stories.

Printed in Great Britain
by Amazon

70978766R00139